The Terrible Silence of God

The Terrible Silence of God

JEFF CARTER

RESOURCE *Publications* · Eugene, Oregon

THE TERRIBLE SILENCE OF GOD

Resource Publications
An Imprint of Wipf and Stock Publishers
199 W. 8th Ave., Suite 3
Eugene, OR 97401

www.wipfandstock.com

PAPERBACK ISBN: 979-8-3852-5094-3
HARDCOVER ISBN: 979-8-3852-5095-0
EBOOK ISBN: 979-8-3852-5096-7

For Tiffini – You help fill the silences in my life. I love you.

In Silence

Behind the electrical hum
of fluorescent bulbs and
radio static is silence;
I'm listening for salvation

like a toppled wall,
a battered fence,

I am a breath, an illusion,
something even lighter
than a breath

I heard you once,
twice, I'm sure of it.

—PSALM 62

Foreword

I'VE BEEN RESEARCHING THE events at the Zion's Freedom compound for most of my adult life, trying to understand what happened there and why. The first of those questions is more straightforward—but by no means simple. The facts are easily stated. The events are easily ordered—though, again, some are contested. The second of those questions is more difficult to answer. Why? Why is always difficult to determine.

But it's not a topic that generates much interest. People still talk about the fiery deaths at the Branch Davidian compound in Waco, Texas of the seventy-six followers of Vernon Wayne Howell, who was better known to the world as David Koresh. But few remember the similar events and deaths that occurred almost nine hundred miles west of and two years before Waco. There are several reasons that the tragedy in Superior, Arizona didn't receive the fury of national and international news media attention that Waco received. For one thing, the siege was shorter, lasting only two days instead of the fifty-one days at Waco. And there were, fortunately, fewer deaths at the Zion's Freedom compound. But that doesn't make it any less tragic. The death of even one individual would have been a tragedy and should be remembered. The death of thirty-one people, including seven children, is horrifying. The fact that these deaths are largely forgotten is unforgivable.

So why did it happen? What triggered it all? What started the fire that incinerated the bodies of thirty-one people—men, women, and children? It's all too easy to blame the FBI and the ATF, though they should certainly share some of the responsibility. But the fire was lit years before they surrounded the Zion's Freedom compound. That fire was lit by their leader, the Reverend DK, who was equal parts self-assured messenger of God, and nervous hustler.

In late 2023 I had the opportunity to finally sit down with Travis Took, the only survivor of the catastrophe. He was only fourteen years old when the bullets and the fire took the lives of his fellow members of the religious movement in the desert of Arizona. In the intervening thirty-one years, Travis has said little to anyone in the media about his experiences with the Revered DK and the people of Zion's Freedom. Now, for the first time, he's broken his silence and given an exclusive interview about the time he spent there and the tragedy that brought it all to a catastrophic conclusion. It is my hope that his recollections will help answer that question: Why?

-Myron Christopher—Producer

Chapter One

A VOICE FROM THE darkness speaks to me. It is the voice of the producer of this documentary, Myron Christopher. "Can you say your name for the camera?" he says. He and his crew are interviewing me because I was there when the Zion's Freedom compound went up in flames. I was there when the FBI and the ATF surrounded us and held us captive inside our home. I was there at the very end.

"Are you ready to do this, Travis?" Myron asks me. I nod and turn toward the camera. The lights are bright and they hurt my eyes.

"My name is Trav. . . " I begin, but Myron cuts me off.

"No," he stops me. "Don't look directly at the camera. Look over here at me."

"Okay," I say and turn on the stool where I'm sitting so that I am facing him. The lights are less intense this way. I can stop squinting and relax.

"Go ahead when you're ready. Tell us your name and we'll get started." Myron is always encouraging me like that. He is easy to talk to. And he is patient. He doesn't yell like other people do. Others around me always seem to be yelling and I don't like that.

"Sure. Okay. My name is Travis Thompson Took. Some folks call me Triple-T," I answer his question and ask one of my own. "Is this going to be part of your documentary? Part of the film that you're making?"

"It is," he says. "We want to get a feel for what it was like there at the camp. We want your impressions, your memories. The story of Reverend DK and the Zion's Freedom compound is often forgotten, overshadowed as it was by the larger, more visible disaster that happened shortly after with David Koresh at the Branch Davidian complex in Waco, Texas. We want to tell the story of Reverend DK and since you're the only survivor of the catastrophe and the fire, you're the only one who can give us a first person, eyewitness account of what happened during those days and what it was like in the Freedom compound with Reverend DK. Hopefully you can corroborate what we know and bring new light to the questions that we have about what happened and why."

I nod my head. This is why Myron's here. And why I'm here. I promised him that I would tell him my story.

"To begin, can you tell me who gave you the nickname, Triple-T, Travis?" Myron asks from the darkness.

"It was Revered DK who called me that when I joined the Zion's Freedom camp. He called me that the whole time I was with them. It's what he called me just before he killed himself so that he could go into the heavens without experiencing another earthly death."

"He killed himself so that he wouldn't experience earthly death?" Myron asks. It sounds like he doesn't believe me.

"Well that's how he put it before he put the shotgun under his chin and pulled the trigger."

* * *

The Superstition Mountains rose almost vertically from the flat Arizona desert plains east of Phoenix, sandy red stone jutting into a sky that was still dark from a rare passing rain, jutting into a sky like slate, like steel. Heavy. Solid. And though the dry heat would soon return, the air for the moment was still cool and moist, the red soil of the ground still wet and dark with moisture. The smell of desert rain is peculiar—dusty, earthy, like pine, like sage. Even though this was a desert, the air after the rain smelled of fecundity, like life ready to bloom. A bald-headed, black vulture swooped over the cliff face, searching for prey. It would eat any carrion it found, but it was also prepared to attack and kill a skunk, or an opossum, or a small pig, or even a stray goat, or lamb.

The area around the mountains had at one time been granted to the Apache tribe as a permanent reservation. But, as it was in every such case, when silver and copper were discovered in the area, that permanently granted reservation was quickly rescinded and the Apache people were forced to relocate once again. This they were unwilling to do and they put up a fierce and bloody resistance. In 1872, at the height of the American Indian Wars, America's longest war, a resolute band of Apache horsemen who'd fought a losing battle against the military might of the US government were ambushed by a cavalry unit. The Apache band quickly lost somewhere between fifty and seventy-five men (the local stories vary somewhat) and began a ragged retreat up that sacred mountain to a place that is now known as the "Apache Leap." Local legend says that the overwhelmed Apaches knew that they were defeated, but instead of surrendering themselves to their enemies, they leapt from the top of that mountain, nearly five thousand feet, to their deaths rather than accept the humiliation of capture.

That's the story that the locals tell. They also go on to say that when the women of the Apache tribe later went to the base of the mountain to find the bodies of their unsurrendered warriors, they wept great tears of anguish and despair. And those tears, when they hit the sand, became black obsidian. The Apache women gathered the bodies of their men and vowed that they would never cry like that again. Today you can purchase jewelry—necklaces and earrings of obsidian inlaid in silver - made from these "Apache Tears."

At the foot of the Superstition Mountains was the Apache Shadow Trailer Park where Travis lived. Even after Travis closed the door of the mobile home he shared with his mother he could hear her bawling after him, "Don't you be playin' around with those boys after school, Travis. I want you to come straight home. I'm gonna' need you to help me move that dresser what broke." Travis sighed and turned up the collar of his jean jacket and tossed his long, dirty hair over his shoulder. "Travis? Do you hear me?" his mother called again.

"Yeah, Ma" he yelled back. "I won't."

"What?" he heard her bellowing from inside.

"He opened the door and stuck his head back inside the dimly-lit interior of the trailer. "I said, I won't, Ma. I'll come home after school, like I said I would."

"You're a good son," she said. "And I love you, Travis, but you're forgetful sometimes. You get to runnin' with those boys and you forget your ma."

Travis lived in a trailer beneath the shadow of the Superstition Mountains with his mother at the edge of Superior, Arizona. His dad had run off when he was still pissin' in his diapers. He knew next to nothing about the man who'd fathered him. The few things that he did know about his dad were: One—his name was Willard. Two—he looked like a dime-store version of Robert Redford. He knew that from the one photograph his mother had saved of the man. And Three—he drove trucks. "He drove into town, knocked me up, and drove off again," his mom told him. "Like one of them movie cowboys." His mother, Brenda, had raised him by herself, alone for fourteen years. And all that time she hadn't brought home any boyfriends. No "uncles." No stepfathers. It was just Travis and his mother against the world.

But these days she couldn't offer much help in their struggle against the world. She'd gained a lot of weight over the years and now, while she wasn't morbidly obese, she still had trouble getting around. Standing up was difficult for her and she had a cane to help with her walking. Some days a social worker from the county would come out to help Brenda get into town for groceries or other errands. But most days she didn't walk any further than from the back bedroom to the living area at the front of the trailer. That's where she watched TV during the days. Sometimes she slept there on the couch instead of walking back to her bedroom. She just didn't have the energy or the strength to make it.

Travis closed the door again and picked up his bike from the side of the porch where he'd dropped it the evening before, and kicked off toward school. Though he wouldn't actually go to the school. He'd already given up on the benefits of education.

* * *

"I forgot to ask earlier, Travis, how old are you now?" Myron asks abruptly.

"I'm forty-six," I tell him.

"And when did you first meet the Reverend?"

"It was the spring of 1992. That was just after my ma died," I answer after I remember the year.

"That would have been about the time of the riots in L.A. following the acquittal of the police officers who assaulted Rodney King."

"I guess so," I tell him. "I didn't watch the news much then." We've only just started the questions for this interview but already I don't want to answer any more. I don't know what I thought the questions would be. I don't like talking about my ma. But I promised that I'd answer and I do my best to keep my promises. Myron says that the documentary is important. And maybe it's good to talk about these things. Myron says it would be okay.

I've been thinking about my ma for a while now and I've come to realize that as much as I thought I loved her—she raised me after all, and did all that she could for me. And it was her and me alone in the world together—but as much as I loved her, I don't think I ever really knew her all that well. I know that her favorite food was lasagna and I know she wasn't a really great cook. I know that she liked watching Perry Mason reruns and old westerns on the TV. But I don't think I ever really knew her. I have very few memories of anything specific with her. I don't know why. Thinking about her is hard.

* * *

The late afternoon sun still baked the landscape. Travis was plinking beer bottles and pop cans with a BB gun along with his friends in the shadow of a copse of Arizona Pine trees. The Pumpmaster 760 air rifle belonged to his pal, Tim. Tim had brought the gun. Aaron had brought the smokes—cigarettes he'd lifted from his grandmother's purse. Travis had brought the beer. He'd stolen a six pack of Budweiser from the convenience store instead of going to school that morning. The fact that he'd already forgotten his promise to his mother never even occurred to him.

Another green glass bottle shattered under Travis' aim. "Great shot, killer!" Aaron shouted. Travis was four for four shots. Even though it was Tim's gun, Travis was the best shot of the three of them.

"We're going to need to set up more bottles," Tim said.

"Take this one," Travis said as he finished off the last swig of his beer, then tossed the bottle overhand at Tim. Aaron laughed and threw his at Tim as well.

Tim swore at the boys and flipped them his middle finger but he gathered up the empties and raced them to the end of their improvised shooting berm. "Keep that gun down while I'm out here," he shouted over his shoulder. "We gotta' practice some goddamn firearm safety, boys!" They all laughed.

The process of setting up a new batch of bottles involved much swearing and laughter as the bottles would not balance easily on the broken and toppled pine logs they were using to hold their targets. The bottles and cans tipped over repeatedly, but Tim eventually got them set up and ran back to the other boys. "My turn," he said and snatched the gun from Travis.

He pumped the BB gun several times and sighted down the barrel at the bottles at the far end of the range, readying himself to take a shot. Just then, before he could pull the trigger again, a brown Highway Patrol car pulled up trailing a fanned spray of dust. A state trooper dressed in his tan uniform stepped out of the car and put on his peaked hat. The boys hastily flicked away their cigarettes behind their backs without any consideration of accidentally starting a wildfire in the dry brush.

"Travis Took, you dumb son of a bitch," the trooper shouted. "Where you been, boy? We've been looking for you all afternoon." Travis didn't say anything but only stared down at the red dirt beneath his scuffed and dirty Converse tennis shoes.

"They sendin' out you highway coppers for truancy now?" Aaron shot back with a loud guffaw.

"You mind that mouth of yours, Aaron Spaulding," the trooper cautioned the boy. "And you too, Timothy Hahn. I know you. I know all three of you boys. And your families too. I bowl with your daddy, Tim." The officer slammed the door of his cruiser. "But I'm not here about your skipping school. And I don't give two farts about the cigarettes and beer I know you've got out here." He turned and looked directly at Travis and spoke gently. "I'm here to pick you up, son. Your momma's been taken to the hospital in Mesa. She's had a stroke, son."

Travis ran past his friends without saying a word to climb into the patrol car with the state trooper. The two of them raced the thirty-five miles on the highway to the hospital in Mesa, Arizona. The officer exceeded the posted speed limits but did not turn on the lights and sirens.

* * *

Brenda died that afternoon, before Travis could arrive in the Highway Patrol car. She died of a stroke. The doctor who spoke to Travis described her death as a cerebrovascular accident. Those words meant little to Travis but he remembered the sound of them and would, in the years afterward, often rehearse them. His mother was dead and he was alone. An agent of the Arizona Department of Child Safety worked with local officials in Superior to arrange for the burial of his mother and told Travis that someone would be reaching out to him in the immediate future to arrange for his placement into a foster home. But, as often happens in overburdened bureaucracies, something went wrong. A file was misplaced or a memo was forgotten, and Travis was forgotten. No one contacted him. No one came for him.

He attended his mother's funeral and the burial that followed at Fairview Cemetery—a miserable, flat patch of land punctuated with tall, darkgreen Mediterranean Cyprus trees. They were solemn trees, appropriate to grief and mourning, commonly known as "drama trees" because of their tendency to bend even in the slightest of breezes. The Methodist minister officiating the burial, the state trooper who'd driven him to the hospital, and Travis were the only ones in attendance as Brenda was lowered into the Arizona ground.

And then he was alone. He stayed in the trailer by himself watching TV late into the nights. He cooked boxes of macaroni and cheese until the milk ran out. Then he ate dry cereal and microwaved popcorn washed down with Pepsi cola. He didn't go to school. He didn't hang out with his friends. He stayed in the trailer and watched television until the food and soda ran out.

When the fridge was empty except for a few unidentifiable masses that had once been vegetables, and the pantry was bare, Travis decided that if he wanted to eat it was time to pick up some groceries. But he didn't have any money for food. He didn't have money for anything. But he wasn't worried. He'd been shoplifting little things since he was twelve—candy, and small toys at first. Later he pilfered more mature things like beer, and cigarettes, and Playboy magazines. He'd been picked up by the police for it a few times, but he'd pretty much perfected his technique by now, and he felt confident that he could swipe some chicken from the grocery store. He wasn't as confident that he could cook it, but he would worry about that later.

At the grocery store he strolled quickly though the aisles to the meat department in the back of the store. The lights were dimmer there. A number of the fluorescent bulbs were either burnt out or flickering. When no one was looking he slipped a package of chicken drumsticks into his jacket and turned to leave the store surreptitiously. He might have made it out of the store except that a woman who was digging in her purse for her checkbook instead of watching where she was going bumped into him as she came into the store. She collided with Travis near the front registers and the chicken slipped away from him. The foam tray of chicken wrapped in plastic bounced and skittered on the ground in front of him. A sharp-eyed clerk saw the collision and the subsequent revelation of pilfered meats and in a flash she'd reached out and snatched hold of Travis' collar and shouted for security.

"That won't be necessary," an authoritative voice announced. "He's with me."

Travis squirmed beneath the grasp of the clerk with quick reflexes, trying to see who was speaking now. He saw a tall, gangly man with large, dark sunglasses perched on an aquiline nose that was more than slightly curved. His face was tanned and his hair was cropped short.

"This boy's with you?" the clerk huffed in disbelief.

"Yes," the eagle faced man said. "I'm sorry for the confusion. There seems to have been some sort of mix up, and that's probably my fault. I told the boy to get the chicken and wait for me up front here by the registers. I was grabbing a few other things." He pulled a folded wad of bills from the pocket of his leather jacket. "I'll pay for everything—the chicken and the rest of this as well."

Having mollified the clerk and paid for Travis' chicken and his own groceries, the man with the sharp nose stood in the parking lot of the grocery store with Travis. He took off his sunglasses revealing a pair of large brown eyes that were so bright they were almost orange. He smiled and said, "My name's DK and I know who you are. You're Travis, right? Travis Took? Your mom just died?"

Travis didn't say anything.

"You live over in the trailer park and your mom just died. And I'd bet that you're hungry."

Travis still said nothing.

"Well, Travis, if you want to come with me, some of the ladies at my church will cook up that chicken for you, set you a proper meal." DK extended his hand holding the plastic bag that contained Travis' chicken.

"What do you want?" Travis asked suspiciously. "Are you one of those kiddie pervs?"

"Not at all. The only thing I want is to make sure that you get fed tonight," DK told him.

Travis looked this supermarket savior over and then said, "I like your sunglasses."

"Well," DK grinned. "It's like the song says, right?"

"What?"

"Cheap sunglasses. . . "

"I don't get it," Travis said.

"Nevermind," DK said. "Hop on," he said pointing to a well-traveled Honda Rebel motorcycle. "Don't worry. I know it's old and it's seen a lot of miles, but it'll get us where we want to go."

"Where's that?" Travis asked.

"Home."

CHAPTER ONE

***

"What were your first impressions of Zion's Freedom?" Myron asks from the darkness beyond the camera.

"What do you mean?" I ask him. I'm not sure what he wants to know. "Do you mean the buildings or the people who lived at the compound?"

"Let's start with a physical description of the camp," Myron says. "We'll layer your descriptions over some of the archival photos we have of the compound."

"Well, at first I thought the place was sorta' run down. I didn't see anyone at all when we came through the gates. I thought maybe he'd lied to me about having a church up there and that he was one of those child molesters after all. It was just all these trailers, like the one I lived in, but different colors and all run together. One was green and black striped. One was bright red like a barn. One was painted with overlapping yellow and orange circles. And they all had Bible phrases painted on them. Some of them were stacked on top of each other with ladders and stairs and platforms. They were all a bit down. Sorta' sorry looking. But they'd built a kind of watchtower at one corner, and that was pretty cool. You could see over the whole compound from there. I used to go up there to watch the sun set sometimes. And the whole compound was backed up against the side of the mountain, with an overhang of rock that came out over the top of some of the trailers. It looked really cool, like a castle, or a fort, or something. They had a flag with a light-blue star on it flying from the watchtower. But it looked empty when we first got there."

"But it wasn't though, was it? Empty I mean . . . "

"No."

"In fact, by the time you joined DK's group in the spring of 1992, there were approximately thirty members in the sect, including the children, right?"

"What's a sect?"

"A religious group, or movement. Some people use the word cult."

"Oh. Well it wasn't a cult. We never called it a cult." I'm surprised that Myron's forgotten. We talked about this when he contacted me about doing this interview. "We always called it the community. Or the family. Never a cult."

"I understand. It was like a family, wasn't it, Travis?" Myron says to me.

"Yeah. We talked a lot about family while I was there."

* * *

As DK parked the small motorcycle behind a row of joined together trailers, a thin woman with ash-blond hair so pale it was almost gray, came out to greet them. She smiled and waved when she saw DK. "I thought I heard that bike of yours," she said with a wry, annoyed smile. "You know that motorcycle is going to be your death, right? They're dangerous. They're death machines."

"Now, Maggie, you know I have no fear of death. . . " DK tried to allay her concern, but she continued her harangue right over the top without regard for his conciliatory words.

"No. I mean it, DK. They're dangerous. And you go rip roaring around on the highway without even so much as a helmet. It's not safe. People get killed on those things every day and I'm afraid that you're going to get hurt sooner or later." She paused and took a long breath, then turned and looked at Travis. "I'm sorry. I shouldn't blow up at you like that. Especially in front of guests. But I just worry about you. I'll stop now. I'll stop. But tell me, who is this handsome young man that you've brought home with you?"

DK introduced him. "Maggie, this is my new friend, Travis. He'll be joining us for dinner."

"And then?" she asked with a grin that Travis didn't understand.

"And then. . ." DK said, "Well after that, we'll just have to see what happens as it happens. Nothing more has been revealed to me yet."

"Is he the one you told us about? The one who you . . . ," Maggie began to ask, but DK pulled down his sunglasses and glared at her. She stopped her question before she could ask it. Maggie nodded to DK and then spoke to Travis. "Is there anything special you would like for dinner? We can cook up just about anything you'd could think of. Do you like spaghetti? Or pizza?"

Travis held the plastic bag with the chicken. "Can you do fried chicken?" he asked almost afraid to hope.

"Fried chicken? Fried chicken is my specialty," Maggie grinned as she took the bag of chicken from him and carried it inside the building. Her shoulder length hair bounced as she walked away.

"That's Maggie Snow," DK told Travis. "She's been with us for about a year now. She and her daughter, Gracie. Gracie is probably with Miss

12

Louisa and the other children. We have our own school for the little ones. We're our own self-sufficient community out here. One happy, healthy little family."

"What's DK stand for?" Travis asked him.

DK laughed. "You might think that everyone would ask me about that, but I think you're the first." He laughed again. "I used to love the game Donkey Kong. I spent a lot of quarters on that arcade game. I was never very good at it though, but I just kept plugging quarters into the machine. One of my friends said that I was as stubborn as that stupid, barrel tossing gorilla and the name just sorta' stuck."

"But, I mean, what's your real name?" Travis asked again.

DK's smile retracted a bit. "I've been called by a lot of names over the years by those that trust and love me—and some of those names have been true. And I've been called by a lot of names by my enemies too. Many of those names have been ugly and mean—but perhaps some of those names were true as well," he said. "But you're right. DK's not the name that my mother put on my birth certificate, but it's the name that most people call me. At least for now. People change and sometimes their names change with them."

"That's cool, I guess," Travis said. And then, "But how did you know my name?"

"I know a great many things, Travis. Things that others don't know and can't know because they've not been revealed to the world. But the fact that I know your name is no real mystery. I've seen you around town. I noticed you. And I met your mother a while back at the laundromat. We got to talking while the laundry ran. She showed me a picture of you. She told me that you were a good son. I could tell that she was really proud of you. Then I saw in the newspaper that your momma died. That's a hard loss, son. I'm sorry."

Travis kicked at the dirt. "I was hanging out with my friends, Tim and Aaron, when she died," he said without looking up. "I told her I'd come home after school to help her move a broken dresser, but I lied. I didn't even go to school that day. We just spent the day riding around on our bikes and shooting Tim's BB gun. She'd been having headaches all week. I should have. . ."

DK took off his sunglasses and interrupted him. "I'm going to stop you there, son. You've gotta' be careful with those 'I should have' statements. What you should have done and what you could have done are two very different things. They don't intersect at all. Even if you had been there with her, what could you have done? Do you recognize the signs of a stroke? Do you know what to do to help someone who's having one? Are you a trained medical professional?"

"Well, no. . . ," Travis mumbled.

"What happened to your mom isn't your fault and there's nothing you could have done to stop it. Some things are written into the book of heaven with indelible ink and they cannot be erased. They can't be changed or altered in any way. Not by me. Not by you. Not by anyone. Now you might feel a twinge of guilt for having lied to her and having broken your promise to her. But you couldn't have stopped her death even if you had been there. And you can't bring her back from that death. That's another of those unchangeables. But you can work on your feelings of guilt and grief. That is something you can deal with."

"I do feel bad," Travis said. Tears were forming at the corners of his eyes. "I shouldn't have been goofing around with the guys. I should have been there to help her with the dresser."

DK put his hand on Travis' shoulder. "The past is gone and it can't be changed. The only thing we can change is the future."

Travis looked up from the ground into DK's large, bright eyes. "I'll keep my promises." Travis vowed. "I won't disappoint anyone like that again. Never."

DK pulled Travis close, wrapping both arms around him in a warm embrace and said, "Your mom would be proud of you, boy. She was right when she said that you're a good son. You are a good son. I knew it even before I met you. You're a good son, and don't you forget it." The tears in Travis' eyes now spilled out and ran down his face.

* * *

[From a transcript of a cassette tape recording of Reverend DK sermon—April 1992]

[Reverend DK] Where do you come from, Murderer? And where are you going, Vagabond? Wandering Tramp? These were the questions I heard echoing in my soul. These are the questions that came to me in the darkness of my life. I didn't know it then, but it was the voice of the Spirit asking those questions. It was the breath of God blowing into the depths of my soul.

And no one could have known who I was then because I didn't even know myself yet. I hadn't realized who I was and who I had been. And there was no way I could have known then who I would become. I was depressed and lonely. I was frightened and angry. I'd locked myself away from the world. And I was drinking gin and rum to silence the voice that asked those questions. And when the liquor didn't work, I tried other chemistries. I tried to silence those ceaseless questions with drugs like heroin and barbiturates.

You see, while I could hear the questions, over and over again in my mind, while I could hear that unceasing voice, I wasn't ready to answer those questions. I was unprepared to listen. I could hear but I wasn't listening. Do you get that? Do you hear what I'm saying? Are you listening to me? Do you hear what I'm saying?

In order to really listen I had to recognize who I was in God. That was the first thing. I had to learn to see beyond myself in order to fully understand myself. I had to receive the Spirit of God in order to understand the gifts of God. No, this isn't human wisdom. This is the Spirit. There is no other way to interpret the spiritual realities. Everything that is done is done for judgment and it is the spiritual man that will judge all things. But the spiritual man cannot be judged by anyone. Remember that. Write it down for it is true.

And you—where are you going, you murderers and vagabonds? Dominated as you are with wicked desires, where are you going? You have no discrimination. You are enslaved by your ignorance. Stupidity's not a sin and there's no shame, no sin in ignorance, except for those who are willfully ignorant. I used to be ignorant myself. I had to learn. I had to change. I had to learn faith. And faith cometh by hearing, and hearing by the word of God. Is it true?

[Voice from the congregation] It is true. Praise God. Amen.

[Reverend DK] What I have come to understand is that I have passed from death into life again and again—because I have learned the love of God. He who doesn't love lives in death. It sounds like a contradiction, doesn't it? A paradox. But it's true. The one who doesn't love lives in death. Whoever hates his brother is a vagabond murderer. Like Cain. And you know as well as I do that no murderer can have eternal life living in him.

I remember so many things. I remember standing under a blinding sun in front of the pyramids of Kufu at Giza in Egypt. I saw stones weighing seventy tons being hauled into place to build a burial tomb. I remember the Apostle Paul and his receding hairline. I remember fire falling from the sky for the annihilation of nations. I remember snarling dogs behind dubious fences. I remember eating cow dung and tufts of grass after the fire. I remember the crucified dead left on the Mount of Olives as a warning to the rest of us. I remember the star that came out of Jacob, Simon Bar Kochba and his brief second war against the imperial forces of Rome. I remember so many things.

And it was a long time before I could understand what all of this meant. It took me a long time to understand, to fully realize the truth of it—that I have lived and died and lived and died and lived again and again and again.

[Unidentified voice from the congregation] If you've lived before, are you Jesus returned to us?

[Reverend DK] I have lived before, it's true. Many times. But no. No. No. Never think it. Jesus is the only begotten. Jesus is the Word of God. And I am not Jesus, and I don't want you to worship me. You should only worship God and God alone. That's the first and greatest commandment, and don't you forget it.

I am not God. I am not Jesus. I am not the Word of God. No. If I am anything I am the Silence of God. Before and after the word is spoken, there is silence. The word comes from silence and returns to silence. A word is spoken and then it is gone. It has a beginning and an end. The syllables are heard and then cease to be heard, the second after the first, the third after the second, and so on in order until the last. After all the others and after the last there is me. There is silence. But the words are pronounced in time, with the eternal word which is in silence. These words are far beyond me. Indeed they are not at all because they pass away and disappear—but the Silence of God endures forever.

Silence is the brother of all things born into the abyss. Before God spoke creation into existence there was silence. And that silence was good and that silence was me. Before the world was created, calm and silence reigned. Nothing existed except that silence. The face of earth was unseen. There was only the motionless sea, and the great emptiness of sky. It was night and silence stood in the dark.

And so we are called to listen for the silence which is with God and through which all things are spoken eternally. How happy, how blessed, are those who have ears to hear the words of the teacher. But happier still, and more blessed are those who have ears to hear and the minds to appreciate the true silence of eternity. Amen.

[End transcript]

Chapter Two

TRAVIS AND DK RETURNED to the trailer Travis had shared with his mother in one of the Zion's Freedom camp's battered pickup trucks. Coming back to the Apache Shadow Trailer Park after the funeral was like entering an unfamiliar city, like traveling in a foreign country. Though he'd grown up there he no longer recognized the place. He'd been up and down those streets all his life but maybe he'd never really seen them. He'd never noticed the suffocating way the trailers were compacted on the lot. One hundred and thirty sun-bleached trailers in various stages of broken disrepair. All the trailers were that way—paint peeling and stairs sagging away from sloped porches, windows broken out and replaced with sheets of plywood. He saw the rusted out cars and the forgotten children's toys left in the yards and wondered who they belonged to. They turned the corner and came round to the trailer, number fifty-seven, that he'd shared with his mom, and he saw a black and orange FOR RENT sign posted in the cracked front window that was yellowed with years of unwashed grime, and a mound of garbage and furniture piled out in front of the trailer.

The Took's furniture had been dumped in a heap at the corner. A ratty couch with multiple cigarette burns, a couple of aluminum kitchen chairs, a ripped mattress that had been twice repaired with duct tape, all of it unceremoniously tossed out for the garbage collectors. When he got out of the truck, Travis discovered his Batman movie poster had been torn from the wall of his bedroom and tossed in among the mess, and that his clothes had been gathered into a pair of black garbage bags and tossed on top of the pile.

Turning away from the heap, the two of them walked up the steps of the porch and found that a new front door had been installed on the trailer and that the door was secured with a shiny new lock. "What's going on?" Travis asked aloud, shocked and confused. "What's happening?"

Just then Mrs. Willa, a neighbor who frequently walked her wiry ter-rier named Bonzo up and down the row of trailers, passed by and saw them trying the door. "Trailer park supervisor was here yesterday. Did all that," she called out from the sidewalk. "Said your momma ain't paid her rent or lot fees for a couple of months. He's gonna' rent it out to someone else. Says he's already got another lessee lined up."

"He can't do that," Travis bawled. "He can't just kick me out of my house, can he? This is where I live."

DK grimaced. "I'm sorry, son, but I think maybe he can."

Travis looked back to the sidewalk to ask Mrs. Willa a question, but she and her ugly little dog had already moved up the road.

"Do you have other family?" DK asked Travis. "Is there anyone else you can live with?"

"No. Dad ran off when I was little," Travis said quietly. "Mom has. . . had a sister somewhere in Chicago. I think. But I haven't heard from her in years and wouldn't know how to get ahold of her anyway. I don't want to live with her. I don't really know her."

Silence filled the space between them. "I've got nowhere to go," Travis said after a moment. "I've got no one." DK said nothing. He just waited into the silence. Then Travis said, "I don't have anywhere else I can go. Can I come stay with your family at the compound?"

"Of course," DK beamed. "Of course. There's always room for another friend at the Zion's Freedom camp."

* * *

"We had a dog there," I say to Myron, but I don't know why I bring it up. I haven't thought about that dog for years. "He used to run around the property chasing squirrels, and chipmunks, and lizards."

"Oh yeah? What was his name?"

"We called him Perro."

"Perro? That's funny," Myron says, but I don't get it. "Perro is Spanish for dog," he explains. "You named your dog Dog." And I laugh 'cause that is funny.

"What happened to Perro?" Myron asks.

"I don't know. I think he ran away when the compound was invaded. I didn't see him in the confusion after. At least. . . I hope he got away."

"Tell me about some of the people you met at the Zion's Freedom compound," Myron says. "Tell me about your relationships with them."

This makes me smile. But it also makes me sad too. I miss my friends at Zion's Freedom. I wasn't there long, but the people I met there were my best friends. Other people—detectives and journalists—have asked me about DK and what happened at the end there, but Myron is the first to ask me about the others. In thirty some years, he's the only one to ask me about them.

"What about Jimmy Wolf?" I say. "Maybe I could tell you about him?"

"Well, what about Jimmy Wolf" Myron says back. "Go ahead and tell me about him."

"His real name was Virgil. But he hated that name. Everyone just called him Jimmy. He always had questions for Reverend DK. Like this one time, during Bible study Jimmy Wolf stood up and said, 'All your experiences, Reverend DK, they don't add up. Can't add up. You're not old enough to have done even half the things you've claimed that you've done.' Jimmy Wolf was always challenging DK like that."

"What kind of things had DK claimed to have done?"

"He said he'd read some Italian book about Marco Polo when he was six and memorized the entire Bible by the time he was eighteen years old. He told us that he'd been a carpenter and a musician in Nashville. Said that he had a recording contract all set up and that he was going to be a rock star, but he gave that up to follow God instead. He told us that he'd ridden his motorcycle across the country, twice back and forth. Said he'd been a pilot in the Bahamas. There was a lot more. All kinds of things."

"Did he ever tell you about the time he was a dance instructor in Wabash, Indiana?"

"Other people have told me about that, but I don't know if I believe them."

"It's true," Myron tells me. "We have his employment records. He worked at an Arthur Murray Dance Center. While he was there he persuaded a number of the bored and lonely housewives who came in for dance lessons to give him substantial amounts of money. According to these women, he was very charming and spoke to them about the mysteries of heaven, but he wasn't a very good dancer. The studio must have agreed with them because he only worked there a few months before he was fired."

"Well, like I said, he never told us anything about being a dance instructor. And I never saw him dance."

"Okay. Okay," Myron says. "Eventually he must have discovered that there were easier ways to make a living than to work long hours in an office, or a dance studio, or a lumber yard. And he didn't trouble himself much about whether it was right or wrong. That would have been irrelevant to the budding prophet. He just said, 'This is what I want to do,' and he did it."

Myron stops and sighs. He apologizes and begins again. "What happened when Jimmy Wolf asked your Revered DK about all his accumulated life experiences?"

"DK told us that he was older than we knew. That he had lived many lives. Both in this life and before this life."

"And what happened to Jimmy Wolf?"

"He died."

"But not in the fire, right?" Myron says.

"No. He died before that. He had a heart attack and died."

"Can you tell me about that?"

"That was the night Jimmy asked why Revered DK was so down on wine and cocktails but allowed that we could drink beer at the compound."

"And what did he say?"

"He quoted a verse from the Bible that says that wine is a mocker and strong drink is a mocker and whosoever is deceived by them is not wise. He said that beer usually has a low alcoholic content so it's not a 'strong drink' like whiskey or wine. Jimmy Wolf couldn't let it go, though, and quoted back another part of the Bible—from Proverbs, I think—that says 'Give strong drink to the one who is perishing and wine to those in distress.'"

"And what did the Reverend DK say to that?"

"He said that he knew that verse as well. But he said, 'Are you perishing, Jimmy Wolf? Are you dying right here, right now tonight? Is that it? If you're dying tonight, I suppose you can have that glass of rum, or gin, or whiskey. Go ahead. Are you dying tonight?' And then he did."

"Did what?"

"Died. He fell over and died right there in the chapel. Heart attack. Someone called 911 and the ambulance came out but it was already too late for Jimmy Wolf. DK said that he wasn't ready to receive the truth. He wasn't ready and that's what killed him."

"That's intense," Myron says.

"Yeah. But DK said not to worry because Jimmy could and would start over. That he wasn't lost forever."

"What happened then?"

"Well the ambulance arrived. And the police too. DK ducked into the back room on the far side of the compound and said not to say anything about him to the police."

"Why would he say that?"

"He told us that it was because he wasn't ready. His time had not yet come."

"What do you think he meant by that, Travis?"

"I don't know."

"Okay. Okay. Is there anyone else you'd like to talk about? What about one of the women?"

I think for a moment and then say, "Well there was Maggie. . . I mean, Ms. Snow. And her little girl, Gracie. Ms. Snow had been thrown out of her house and home by her husband. Her ex-husband, along with Gracie, who wasn't much more than a toddler at the time. He'd hurt them both. Abusive, you know. DK found her crying at the street corner and offered her a ride, and then a place to stay, just like he offered me. She didn't have anything more than the clothes she was wearing when DK found her. But the ladies at the Freedom camp took her in just like she was one of their own. And everyone loved Gracie. You couldn't help but love her. She was a beautiful little kid. The people at the Freedom camp said that DK was always bringing home strays like that."

I smile at this memory. I loved Ms. Snow and Gracie and I miss them. I miss them a lot. They were pretty and nice. Gracie always made everyone laugh. She was so funny.

"Tell me more about Maggie and Gracie," Myron says, but I don't want to say anything more about them.

"I don't want to talk about them anymore."

"Why not? It seems like Maggie was really important to you. And I can tell that you loved them, especially Gracie . . ." But I just shake my head. It hurts too much to think about them, and it makes me sad. I don't like thinking about them. "Do you want to take a break?" Myron asks. "We can stop Have a drink of water and then come back to them. . . "

"Can we just move on?" I say. I really don't want to talk about them anymore.

"Sure thing, Travis," Myron says. "Let's try a different question. Did DK ever tell you his real name?"

I grin. "Yeah. Yeah he did. It was Sixten. Sixten Everett Johnson." I laugh a little. It's a funny name.

"Sixten's not exactly a common name, is it?" Myron says.

"He said it was a Viking name that meant Stone of Victory. He told me that when we went to Texas for the guns."

* * *

[From a transcript of a cassette tape recording of Reverend DK sermon—April 1992]

[Reverend DK] Real life is meaningless, right? You know this. It's nothing more than a relentless stream of experiences from birth to death, one thing after another, after another, after another. You get up in the morning. You get dressed. You go to work. You come home after work. You eat dinner. You watch some television. Maybe you make love to your wife, or to your husband and then you go to sleep. Rinse and repeat. Day after day, after day until you die. We are wounded in birth and bleed to death. One of the poets said that, I think. Birth is nothing but death begun.

And there's no meaning in any of it. Nothing. This life is, or can seem to be, just an unending succession of physical events. This happens, and then this happens, and then this happens, and then this, and this and this, on and on until you die. But don't get me wrong. I'm not one of those existentialists. I'm not a nihilist who believes that life is absolutely meaningless and that human knowledge is impossible. I can see that some of you were getting a little concerned. Weren't you?

[Nervous laughter from several individuals among the congregation]

[Reverend DK] But that's what it can feel like, right? Meaningless. We're bored. We're tired. And we're tired of the banality of it all. So we try different things to stave off the boredom. Right? Some of us try booze and drugs thinking that there might be some relief at the bottom of the bottle or in the tip of the syringe. But there's no relief there. I can tell you that. Some of you know it from your own lives. I know. I know. But you can forget the booze and the pills.

Others go shopping. Yeah, shopping. The commercials you see on TV and hear on the radio tell you that you'll be happy and satisfied and fulfilled if you have a new wardrobe or a new, larger appliance, or a faster computer, or a flashier car. But you are more than a consumer. You are not what you wear. You are not what you buy. Commercials are lies. Get out of that world. Get out of the mall. Forget the mall because the mall can't fill that void that you're feeling.

Some try to hide the meaninglessness in their lives with food, or sex, or by watching movies, or lifting weights. Or sports. Or travel. You name it, someone's tried it. And none of these things are bad in and of themselves. But they're just another set of physical sensations in an endless sequence of physical sensations. You can't cover over meaningless existence with more meaningless experiences. You can't get something from nothing. There has to be something else. Something more. Something real.

It is faith that gives us a frame upon which to hang all these meaningless experiences. It's faith that gives us a way to create order from the chaos, the same way that God called forth order from the welter and waste, the formless void that existed before creation. Not booze. Not pills. Not eating. Not sex. It's faith that gives our lives meaning. And you can have faith in me. I know your fears. I can see through your mind. I know your dark feelings. But trust me. Believe in me. Have faith in me—because all of my feelings are good.

[End transcript]

Chapter Three

US. HIGHWAY SIXTY OUT of Superior, Arizona was a two lane, black-topped highway with clear vistas of the mountains and forests to the east. Beyond that lay New Mexico and, further on, the great state of Texas. And the guns were in Texas, just a short, ten hour ride away. DK and Travis roared eastward on the highway on DK's small but sturdy Honda Rebel motorcycle. It was a small bike for such a long ride, but the bike was well built, with a powerful engine that could maintain highway speeds for long periods of time without difficulty. And it was a smooth ride, even through the mountains and the hairpin turns through the Apache National Forest.

Travis enjoyed the ride. He'd never been out of the little town of Superior before. His entire life had been in that little trailer park under the shadow of the Superstition Mountains. Now he was roaring up the highway on a cool bike with a new friend. The sun shone in the clear sky and Travis felt like he was flying over the mountains himself. Like some great bird of prey—a hawk or an eagle—a vulture even, with a wingspan large enough to embrace the entire sky. The wind rippled through his long hair and the vibrations of motorcycle's engine was gentle and soothing. This was freedom. This was living. This was real life. This was the open road into an unknown but glorious future.

"This highway will take us all the way from Arizona, through Quernado, New Mexico where we'll swing north to catch Highway Forty, which will take us through Albuquerque and into Texas," DK told Travis as they examined a battered gas station road map before setting out on their road trip. He pointed out the stretch of blue line that traced across the southwestern corner of the United Sates on the map.

"Can we stop in Roswell while we're in New Mexico?" Travis asked.

DK chuckled. "You want to see flying saucers and the men from Mars, eh? Like Mulder and Scully?" He patted Travis on the shoulder and said,

"Sorry, no. Roswell's too far south to stop there this trip. But maybe we can head down there another time. We can, however, stop in Alaska," he said with a droll, knowing grin.

"Alaska?" Travis asked, surprised.

"Alaska, New Mexico," DK grinned. "It's the halfway point along our route. We'll go that far today and spend the night at Lake Acomita. But don't get your hopes up about the accommodations there. It sounds nicer than it is. Then we'll get up early and finish the rest of the drive to Texas tomorrow morning."

"Alaska, New Mexico. That's funny," Travis said and laughed a short, bright laugh. "Do you think there will be snow?"

"I doubt it," DK smiled. "But weirder things have happened, I suppose." The two of them laughed at the incongruous thought of snow in the middle of the New Mexico desert.

"Tomorrow we'll make our way to a little place called Canyon, Texas. It ain't much of town but there's a giant cowboy statue there that I think you'll like. And Georgia O'Keeffe spent a few years there."

"Georgia O'Keeffe? Who's he?" Travis asked.

"*She* was a modernist painter at the beginning of the twentieth century," DK explained.

"Oh," Travis said, clearly not interested. "And there's a giant cowboy? Will we be able to see it?"

"You can't miss it," DK said.

✳ ✳ ✳

"Oh hey," I have a sudden realization. "That David Koresh guy in Texas . . ."

"Yes," Myron says. "What about him?"

"He and DK have the same initials, don't they?"

"Indeed, they do."

"And they both died in similar way, didn't they?"

"Yeah," Myron agrees and sighs. "There were a number of other similarities—like the fact that both of them gathered a community of devoted followers, both of the purchased illegal firearms, and so on. There were a few other minor synchonicities as well. It's one of those outlandish coincidences that makes it appear as if reality might have some sort of inherit meaning after all. But it's just that—a coincidence. Nothing more. We've looked into it. But our investigation, as well as those conducted by the police and the FBI, have turned up no connection between your Reverend DK and David Koresh of the Branch Davidians down in Waco, Texas. As far as we can determine, they never met, never corresponded. Their paths never crossed and they don't have any shared acquaintances. And there substantial differences between them. For example - there were no allegations of sexual impropriety brought against your DK. None that could be substantiated anyway. He was never accused of breaking up families like David Koresh did at Waco."

"In any case," he continued, "the coincidence of names is only an apparent coincidence since David Koresh was actually born Vernon Wayne Howell and your DK was actually Sixten Johnson. The common initials is simply a meaningless coincidence."

"But with the other similarities and all," I say, "well, it's just sorta' funny, right?"

"Yeah. Funny. Life is funny like that sometimes," Myron says. He chuckles but doesn't sound amused.

* * *

Lake Acomita wasn't exactly a picturesque vacation spot. It was an artificial reservoir behind an aging dam surrounded by barren desert. Even the view of Mount Taylor in the distance did little to enliven the pathetic scrub land. But Travis was thrilled nevertheless. To his eyes the lake was a sparkling jewel of an oasis in the desert and the desert landscape was a vast vista of splendor.

"This place isn't really open for camping," DK said as they got off the bike and stretched their legs. "But we should be okay. If we keep our campfire small, I don't think anyone will notice us here. "The spot he'd found was a secluded, wooded area of pines, firs, and junipers off a gravel road near the lake. "We can run in to town to get something to eat in a little while."

"Don't we need tents or something?" Travis asked. He'd never been camping but he thought they might have been missing a few things.

"I've got a couple of blankets," DK said. "That's all we really need. We'll sleep here under the stars like cowboys or frontiersmen."

"Yeah?" Travis said, still not convinced but willing to believe."

"Do you know the constellations? Orion? Ursa Major? Ursa Minor?"

"I can find the Big Dipper sometimes."

"Well, that's a start," DK said. "Later tonight I can point out some of the other constellations for you. But first, how about we head into Alaska for some dinner?"

"And some snow," Travis said with an unrelenting smile.

"And some snow," DK laughed.

Dinner was greasy burgers and fries, and Travis loved that too. He'd eaten fast food hamburgers before, to be sure. What fourteen year old boy in America hadn't? Even so, this was all new and strange and unfamiliar. Exhilarating.

"I didn't know that ministers could ride motorcycles and wear leather jackets," Travis said around a mouthful of half-chewed burger.

"Exactly how many ministers have you known," DK asked him.

"Well, none," Travis said.

"You've got ketchup on your face, kid," DK said as he tossed a handful of napkins across the table to him.

That night as they sat in the warmth of a small campfire, DK pointed out the constellations for Travis, tracing with his finger the imaginary lines between the stars that made up Ursa Major and Minor, Hydra and Leo. The light pollution in Alaska, New Mexico was minimal so they were able to see nearly the whole expanse of the night sky.

"There must be millions of stars out there," Travis said deep in awe.

"More," DK told him. "Many more. Inconceivably more. Our own Milky Way galaxy contains about four billion stars. And there are billions of galaxies—each of them with that many, or more, stars within them. The number of stars is functionally uncountable. Innumerable, just as the Bible says."

"Whoa. . . "

"But," DK cautioned, "the number of stars that we can actually see with our unaided eyes is around two thousand. Even fewer in and around cities with all their artificial lights." They sat in silence together for a long while, staring at the stars.

"I see something in you, son. Something of myself," DK said after the silence, Travis said nothing but continued staring up at the stars. "You told me that your dad left when you were little. Mine did too. I never knew my father. He left my mother and me before I was even born. And I barely knew my mom. Not until later. She left me with her mother—my grandmother—to raise me. But I didn't know it. I called her 'mom' for years before I knew the truth. My grandfather, who I thought of as my father, didn't want me in his home. He made it clear that I was unwelcome. He never hurt me—not physically, anyway. But he was cruel and he left no doubt that I was unwanted there. So I ran off when I was sixteen. Not much older than you. I've been on my own ever since then, so I know what it's like to be alone."

DK went on. "I'll tell you something more. I've been close to death all my life. I was born prematurely. I was born at only eighteen weeks, far too early to have survived—especially considering the state of medical technology in 1959. Neonatal care was pretty minimal back then. So it's a verifiable miracle that I survived. I was close to death even at my birth. Since then I've had two other NDEs. Do you know what that means?"

"No," Travis said quietly.

"An NDE is a near death experience. What the French refer to as *l'expérience de mort imminente*. I've been clinically dead twice in my life. And I can tell you about those incidences later. I can tell you about the sensation of floating away from my body and ascending into heaven. I can tell you what I saw and what I heard during those experiences. But not tonight. Those are stories for another time. Suffice to say, I think it's this closeness to death that I've had all my life that allows me to see things that others in this life can't see."

"That's weird, man."

"You're telling me," DK said with a slight chuckle. "The visions and flashbacks I have terrified me when I was young—before I understood what I was seeing. Before I understood who I was and who I am. And the voices I heard then have never stopped. I thought I was crazy. Certainly my family thought I was. That's a large part of why my grandfather never wanted me around. He was afraid of my crazy."

"I don't know what any of that means," Travis said. "I don't understand."

"It's okay," DK assured him. "You don't need to understand yet, but one day you will. And then you'll know what it all means."

"Why are you telling me about all this?" Travis asked after a moment of consideration.

"Because," DK said, "as I told you, I see something of myself in you."

"But I don't have any visions. I'm just a kid."

"No. No. No. Don't say things like that. You might not have visions and recollections of other lives in other places like I've had, but you are more—much more than 'just a kid.' There is something special and peculiar about you. Something that needs to be awakened."

"What do you mean? What is it?"

"I don't know yet, but I've seen it. I don't know what it is yet, but I'm sure that it's important. And it's my hope that you and I can be friends so that we can find out together."

* * *

[From a transcript of a cassette tape recording of Reverend DK sermon—May 1992]

[Reverend DK] Write this down—the Lord is dictating words to my mind, and to my heart. The Lord is pressing on my mind. Now, I am not God. Don't be confused about that. Don't get that wrong. I am not God. But I am the silence of God, the silence that comes before and after the spoken word. And I am the voice of God while I am speaking. I can't sit here and tell you that I'm just like you when I am not. I am different. I was born different. I am more. I was born more. I don't belong to this world in the same way that you do. So when I speak to you, you should listen, and hear, and remember. Write this down so that you can think about it and remember it later because it is the word of God coming to you through the silence.

I know your thoughts. I know your deeds. I know your dreams. I know your wishes and your desires. I know you better than you know yourselves. And I will not die—this is how I can know. I will be renewed to be young again. I will live on. And the same is true for you. You will not die, but you will be renewed, reborn to live again. You will live on. And you will know.

We are programmed by our culture to accept death. We live in a culture of death. And I know death. I've lived with death. We are programmed by our culture and society to not only accept death, but also to fear it. I used to fear death, just as I used to fear the coming of the apocalypse. I used to fear the nuclear bomb. I used to be afraid of the terrorists. But I'm not afraid anymore. I mean, it's the 90s, right? The Cold War's over. The Soviet Union is collapsing in upon itself. The Berlin Wall is already down. We're safe now, right? Right? The enemy is gone - or nearly so. We're safe. . . But the threat is still there, of course. Greater than ever, maybe.

But they'll soon have us fearing a new enemy. It's inevitable. That's how they control us—with our fear. If there's not an enemy at the door, they will create one for us to fear. One with terrible weapons and a burning, unquenchable hatred for us. It was the Russians. Now it's the Middle East. We're already at war there in Iraq, right? You can watch it live on CNN twenty-four hours a day. Live from Baghdad. I don't know who the next enemy will be, but there *will* be a new enemy to threaten us. Maybe it will be Russia again. Or maybe China. Who knows? The point is this—there must always be an enemy to fear. That's how they control us.

But the man who isn't afraid, the woman who isn't afraid, is uncontrollable. Ungovernable. Write this down.

I used to be afraid of Cold War nuclear crossfire. I used to worry frequently about nuclear war. But I'm no longer afraid. All the nuclear missiles, all the bombs—they can destroy the world with nuclear flame, but they can't destroy me. They can't destroy you. Because they cannot destroy God and we are living the life of God. That which lives the life of God cannot be killed or destroyed.

So I'm not afraid anymore of Cold War nuclear crossfire. I'm not afraid of Saddam Hussein. I reserve my fear for God and God alone. For he is the Fear of Isaac in this time of Jacob's trouble. The prophet Jeremiah told us about that in his book of Consolations. Jeremiah chapter thirty. We are promised a future and a hope. There will be a time of intense trouble and distress, a time of strong terror and overwhelming awe, but we are promised that the faithful will be saved from it.

[End transcript]

* * *

"Tell me about the guns," Myron says.

"We got those in Texas," I tell him.

"And how did the Reverend pay for them?"

"He paid cash. He had a thick roll of bills. I don't know how much. It was a lot, I think."

"And where did that money come from?"

"The community grew vegetables in a small farm. We had peppers, tomatoes, and eggplants. Things like that. We also had bees for honey and we made soap. We sold those to raise money."

"Yes, but produce and honey and soap . . . could the sale of those account for all the money that the Reverend DK spent on illegal firearms? It was, as you said, a lot of money."

"What do you mean?"

"You couldn't have sold enough eggplants, honey, and soap to account for the weapons the Reverend was buying. Where did the rest of the money come from?"

"I don't know," I tell him because I don't know.

"Didn't the Reverend DK convince members of your community to give him their money and to sell their property and donate the proceeds to him?"

"I don't know. DK never spoke to me about money."

"What about Gideon and Janice Lamont? Do you remember them?"

"I do. They were nice. They had a pet lizard. They let me feed it crickets."

"Before joining the Zion's Freedom camp, they owned a couple of properties in Sedona, Arizona. They sold them and gave the proceeds to your Reverend DK. It was nearly a million dollars."

"I don't know anything about that."

"There are also rumors, unsubstantiated accounts that the Reverend DK was not only buying illegal weapons, but that he was selling them too."

"I don't know anything about that. I've never really thought about it."

* * *

The forty-seven foot tall, concrete statue of a slouching cowboy rose in front of them like a faded Texan vision. Years of wind and blowing sand had faded the once vibrant colors of Tex Randall, the tallest cowboy in Texas. But there he stood, arms akimbo, leaning over a road sign, wearing a ten gallon hat, a bandanna, painted denim jeans, and sporting a bushy mustache.

"That's hilarious," Travis guffawed. "He's awesome."

DK steered the motorcycle between two white cargo vans parked near the base of the cowboy statue and killed the engine. "We're going to meet someone here. He's a friend," DK said. "But we don't trust him. Not completely. So keep your wits about you, son." DK patted Travis on his shoulder and said, "Just follow me."

Just then the driver's door of one of the cargo vans opened and an obese man wearing jeans and a bright yellow and orange Hawaiian print shirt exited. The van rocked and shifted as he removed his weight from the vehicle. His hair was long and thin and greasy. "Well good goddamn," he said, nearly shouting. "It's the Reverend. How the hell are you?" The two of them clapped arms around each other. "And who is this with you?"

"This," DK said, "is my new friend, Travis. We call him Triple-T. He's going to help me get the merchandise home." He turned to Travis and said, "Travis, this is my old friend Mister Harvey."

"Mister Harvey?" the loud, rotund man barked. "Since when did you call me anything but William?" He turned to Travis, "And did the good Reverend here tell you what kind of merchandise you'd be delivering?"

Travis nodded. "Guns."

"Good. Informed consent is the standard of our operation here. I wouldn't want to think that the Reverend was corrupting the youth of America." He smiled expansively. "Not without informed consent, any-ways." He laughed again. Loudly. "I sell guns, young Mister Triple-T. I sell guns because I like guns. I like 'em because they're cool. And I carry one with me every day. A different gun every day," William Harvey said as he flung open the back door of the cargo van and revealed a long, wooden case. "'Ask and ye shall receive,' as your Reverend DK might say. You wanted AK-47s. I got you your AK-47s."

"And they are . . . " DK began to ask.

"Modified?" Harvey finished. "Of course. Of course." He laughed long and loudly. "What fun would they be if they weren't? How many of these cocksuckers did you want?"

"Three," DK said.

"Three?" Harvey objected. "I made the trip all the way out here when it's hotter than a whore's crotch for a measly three rifles?"

"Just three," DK said again, firmly. "That's all I need. This time."

"Okay, okay," the gun dealer sighed. "I've got your three. And, because you're my friend, I got you the van you asked for."

The three of them emptied the motorcycle's gas tank, "So there won't be fumes in the van as we drive home," DK explained. It didn't take long since the tank was nearly empty from the drive into Canyon. After it was dry, they rolled the bike up a ramp made from a plank of weathered lumber. For a moment Travis worried that the sagging plank would snap beneath the weight of the motorcycle and that the bike would fall, crushing him as he tried to keep it aloft. But the plank held, and the bike was safely loaded into the van. They used cargo straps to secure it to the walls of the van—side to side and front to back with a plastic tarp beneath it, "To catch any leaks," DK said. "Just in case."

They wrapped the three illegally modified assault weapons in the blankets they'd used the night before while camping near the lake and put them in the back of the van with the motorcycle.

When they were finished DK went into the gift shop at the base of the giant cowboy statue to use the restroom while Travis waited at the van, drinking a bottle of water. The gun dealer rustled around in the back of his van for a moment and then returned to Travis with a book in his meaty hand. "I want to give you something, kid," he said as he offered the book to him.

"Travis took the book which had a striking red, black, and white cover depicting a man and a woman with firearms. He read the title and the author's name out loud. "The Tuner Diaries by Andrew Macdonald."

"But that's one of them pen names, a what ya' call it, pseudonym," Harvey explained. "His real name's William Pierce. Good man, that one. Great man. You read that and you'll learn a lot about the world." Travis began thumbing through the pages and reading the reviews on the back cover

"Put that down," DK shouted as he crossed the parking lot. "Come on, man! Don't give him that racist crap."

"Okay. Okay," Harvey said. "Christ, man. Just tryin' to broaden the kid's mind."

DK snatched the book away from Travis and thrust it back toward Harvey. "Stick to guns, Mister Harvey, and leave the literature to the librarians."

William Harvey took his book and sulked away to clamber awkwardly back into his van. "Call me when you want more than three of those cocksuckers. "You get home and shoot 'em a few times and you'll be calling me for more," he shouted and then drove away.

DK turned to Travis and said, "Do you know how to drive?"

* * *

Travis drove the van for a couple of hours of the first leg of the return trip to Superior. He began clumsily enough, irritating other drivers who roared by with their horns blaring. He started with jerks and sometimes stopped hard with a screech of tires. "It's a good thing we strapped the bike down," DK said with a grin. But he slowly got the hang of it and was able to drive the van down the highway, using his turn signals to indicate lane changes and maintaining an appropriate distance between other vehicles like a safe driver.

When the highway started up into the mountains, DK took over and did the rest of the driving home. They stopped again in Alaska to camp for the night. And, again, Travis joked about finding snow in New Mexico. And DK laughed again.

The next morning they started out early, driving across the desert. Just after noon, with only an hour more to drive, DK pulled the van off the highway to a scenic overlook near Becker Butte to show Travis the view. Standing at the low, white stone wall that bounded the overlook, Travis gaped at the canyon and the Salt River far below the steep stone cliffs.

"I know that look. I know what you're thinking," DK said to the boy.

"What? What do you mean?" Travis asked.

"You're looking out over that gorge and wondering, right? Wondering what it would be like to jump, right? Just to fling yourself out into the open air. . . "

"Jump?" Travis gasped. "No—I wouldn't."

"Come on, Triple-T. I'm human. You're human. It happens to almost everyone. It's normal. So normal, in fact, that it has a name."

"What is it?"

"The French call it *l'appel du vide*. The call of the void. It's the inexplicable and sudden desire to jump from a high place or to swerve your car into oncoming traffic or into a bridge abutment. A friend of mine has anxiety about crossing long bridges. She worries that she'll get the urge to swerve her car off the bridge and plummet to her death. So I get it. I understand. Here you are—staring into the abyss and the abyss is staring back at you, calling your name. Saying, 'Do it. Be free.'"

"But I'm not. . . "

"You're not suicidal? No. Of course not. You're a perfectly normal fourteen year old boy. These thoughts are spontaneous. They're intrusive thoughts. They just float into your mind. You're not dwelling on thoughts of death. You're thinking about freedom. In a way, it's actually a life affirming thought."

"I could just jump. . . "

"You could be free."

"Free. . . "

A slow breeze blew over them from the depths of the canyon. Suddenly Travis could hear everything in the breeze—the screech of a hawk soaring overhead, the rumble of traffic on the highway, the chirrup of insects in the brush, the gurgle of the Salt River flowing below. He could hear it all. He could smell the asphalt from the roadway and the exhaust of the passing cars. He could smell the dirt and stone from the cliffs, and the pine trees growing on the mountain. He could feel the heat of the sun. He could feel his heart beating. He closed his eyes and took a deep breath and, holding it for a moment, emptied his mind of all conscious thought. He prepared himself for nothingness. For a rush of wind and then oblivion. He prepared himself for silence and darkness forever. The erasure of worry and fear. The cessation of guilt and grief. It was nothing but a leap into the void. A leap not into death—but a leap into God.

"But not today," DK said as he placed his hand on Travis' shoulder. "We have to get back to the Freedom compound."

Travis opened his eyes and released the breath he'd been holding. "Yeah," he sighed and the two of them returned to the van. Neither of them spoke the rest of the way. Instead they listened to the roar of the wind and the highway in the open windows of the van.

✳ ✳ ✳

"Why did the Reverend want the guns, Travis," Myron asks me.

I don't have an answer immediately. It's a question that others have asked me. I told them the same thing that I told Myron and his crew but none of them seem to believe me. "He just though they were cool," I say again to Myron. I don't know what else to tell him.

"Cool?"

"He said it was an intuition. He didn't really know why he wanted them except that he thought they were cool. And that he thought he might need them for something."

"It certainly doesn't seem like he was trying to start a militia—even if he was buying illegal weapons. When investigators examined the evidence after the fire, they only found a few automatic rifles and a couple of handguns."

"And the shotgun," I remind him.

"Yes. The shotgun," Myron says. "The ATF has admitted that he didn't have enough weapons to constitute a real threat. And that he wasn't actively seeking to purchase more. And, as I said, those reports of him selling weapons are completely unsubstantiated."

"Yeah. He just thought they were cool. And he liked shooting them."

"And he thought that he might need them for something."

"Yeah."

"Well he certainly used them at the end, didn't he?" Myron asks. It feels like a dig. Maybe it is.

"Yeah. I suppose he did."

* * *

[From a transcript of a cassette tape recording of Revered DK sermon—May 1992]

[Reverend DK] I am a warrior. I am a warrior for God. And I have fought the armies of Satan not only in this life but in lives before this one. I fought the armies of Satan for millennia in the hostile realms and in the pre-mortal worlds. I am not living in a single dimension. I am living in multiple dimensions. In multiple times. I have lived before. Again and again. And I have battled with demonic forces. I have fought with demons in age after age.

Now some would say that rebirth can only be symbolic. Spiritual. Especially in the west. In western thought we live, we die, and that's it. One shot, then done. It is appointed unto man once to live and die but after this, the judgment. Right? After that it's off to either heaven or hell for all of eternity. But in the east the concept of reincarnation, or the transmigration of the soul is more prevalent. In the east rebirth isn't merely symbolic. 'You must be born again,' is not just a spiritual command. And it's not just the Hindus in India that believe in the eternal rebirth of the soul. You can find that belief among the ancient Greeks, and the Celtic Druids. You can find it in the thirteenth century Jewish book, the Zohar. Even the native peoples of this land where we live now believed in the rebirth of the soul. It's a universal constant.

There is a pattern that remains after we die, an echo of who we were, a few notes of the song that we sang with our lives drifting on the breeze. And the notes of that melody are played again and again, on different instruments. Something remains. We return.

Do you understand what I'm trying to tell you? These are not new things.

Look at the sky. Think of it. All of this was unthinkable before you came to me. It was all unthinkable to you. But now you have changed. You are changing. You are beginning to understand. Before we understand we are unable to trust blind faith. That is why we have to leap. But its not a leap of faith. It is a leap *into* faith. A leap into faith unknowing. These are desperate times, even if, as they constantly assure us, the Cold War is over. These are still desperate times of pestilences and paranoias.

As it is written, 'You shall be hated.' Well we have been hated, haven't we? And we have been rejected too. Right? We have been ignored. We have been cut off. But that's okay. And it's okay that it's not okay. All will be well, and all will be well, and all manner of things will be well. Are there demons from vast, frozen void waiting for me? I've seen them. I know they're there—but are they still waiting to do me harm? It may be that they are, but I am not afraid of them. I have fought with the demons in age after age. I know their tricks. I know how to control them. And you shouldn't be afraid of them either.

Hear me when I tell you these things, people. I am the Silence which is in everything. I am the Silence, and the Silence has gone out from me, and the Silence will come back to me. Can you hear it? If a tree falls in the woods and no one's there to hear it, that's me. If you split a piece of wood—I am there. If you turn over a stone, what do you think you'll find? Me!

You see, I am everywhere and nowhere. I am everyone and no one. I'm not even myself. I am in that space between us and ourselves. You say that you don't know who you are or what you are doing with your lives? I can tell you because I am in that great divide. I am the Silence before and after the words, the Silence between the words. What is it that you hear when I am speaking to you? Soon everyone will hear these things and know what only I know now. But by then it will be too late for them. Anyone who denies the truth of this can bark and bray as much as they like. Let them deafen themselves with their howling, it will make no difference.

[End transcript]

Chapter Four

"MUCH HAS BEEN SAID in other media about what happened at the end at the Zion's Freedom compound, and we'll get to those events ourselves before too long. It's why we're here, after all. But before we get to all of that, I'd like it if you could tell me a bit about your daily life at the compound," Myron says.

"What do you want to know?"

"Tell me what you did and how you lived. The sort of every day life details that can get lost in the high drama of what happened at the end."

"Well one of the things we liked to do was ride the trails around the mountains. We had a couple of ATVs to ride in the compound. Those were fun. We used to ride them up and down the trails. Sometimes we saw bighorn sheep and coyotes. One time we even saw a black bear. That was kinda' scary."

"Maybe you could tell me a story about Ms. Maggie and little Gracie?"

I think about this for a while. I have many stories I could tell about Ms. Snow and her little girl. Like the time that Maggie made a birthday cake for me, with candles and everything. She even piped T-T-T in purple frosting on it. And Gracie blew out the candles for me. "I maked a wish," she said clapping her hands. Everyone laughed because she was so happy. But there are few stories about them that I am comfortable sharing, even with Myron.

Finally I think of one that I can share with him. "One day I found a stray kitten, a little orange kitten with one eye. It had been alone for a while, apparently, and it wandered into our compound by itself. I picked it up and carried it back to the compound's refectory and showed it to Maggie . . . to Mr. Snow. She smiled and gave me a couple of tins of sardines to feed it. Gracie helped me feed it and Ms. Snow named it."

"What did she name the kitten, Travis?"

"Ms. Snow called him Nip."

"Nip?"

"Yeah. Like Cat Nip. . . "

"That's clever," Myron says with a chuckle. "What happened to Nip?"

"I guess he must have died in the fire. I didn't have time to look for him, but . . . "

"But what?"

I can't say anymore. It hurts too much. "Can we move on?" I ask Myron.

"Sure," he says. "Let's try a different question."

"Okay," I say.

"Many of the things that the Reverend DK taught at Zion's Freedom were outside the norm of mainstream Christianity. I'm interested to know just how the Zion's Freedom group went from being an ordinary, if somewhat heterodox congregation of Christian fundamentalists to embracing the Reverend DK's idiosyncratic unorthodoxies. Can you help me understand how that happened?"

I hear the words that Myron is saying, but they don't make any sense. Myron uses a lot of fancy words sometimes and I don't always understand him. "I don't even know what you just said."

"Metempsychosis, also known as reincarnation—the transmigration of the soul, for example, is not part of orthodox Christian theology. But but your Reverend DK made it part of his regular teaching."

"Yeah?"

"And certainly his messianic claims should have raised hackles. . . "

"Raised hackles?" What does that mean? What are you saying?"

"Tell me what it was in Reverend DK's religious instruction that drew you to him. Why did you and the others at the Freedom compound believe in him and accept the strange doctrines that he taught? Did you, yourself, come to believe that you had experienced past lives? Did he help you to remember your previous lives?"

"No. I could never remember any lives before this one. This one's been enough for me. I'm not sure I'd want any more than this one."

"Okay, Travis. Okay. I'm sorry. I just want to understand what happened there. Help me to understand. What about his teaching drew you and the others to him?"

I take time to think about what I will say because I want to answer him honestly. But I don't really understand the question.

* * *

DK and Travis set up for target practice with their newly purchased AK-47s. They lay on a shooter's mat, unfolded and rolled out flat on the rocky ground under the glaring Arizona sun. Travis aimed the rifle down the range toward the paper bull's-eye target they'd set up at the end of the berm.

"Be gentle with it," DK instructed. "You don't want to jerk the trigger back."

DK was prepared to offer more instruction on the proper firing technique of the automatic rifle Travis held in his hands, but he'd already squeezed the trigger three quick times. They looked down the range and saw that two of the three shots hit the target near the center and the third hit in the outermost ring.

"Well," DK said, "It looks like you don't really need my help here."

"Yeah. I like shooting. But I've never shot one of these before," Travis said.

"Well you've certainly got the knack for it, that's for sure. Maybe you were a marksman in another life, or a sniper," DK said with a wide smile and ruffled Travis' hair.

"I don't know . . . " Travis said. "I can't remember any other lifes. Not like the ones you talk about. Sometimes I even have trouble remembering stuff from this life. Like what my mom looked like. Sometimes I can't remember that and other stuff . . . " His voice hitched and his lip quivered.

"Travis, my boy," DK said, enfolding him into an embrace. "Travis, don't you worry none about that. For some people—people like you—it's not the past that's important. For people like you, it's the future that matters. Maybe you haven't experienced any previous lives. I don't know. Not everyone does. But what I do know, and I can know this just by looking at you. I see it in you, son. I can see that your future is bigger and brighter than this life that you know. The lives behind you, if there are any, matter less than the life and the lives ahead of you. Do you understand what I'm saying to you? It's like the prophet says, 'Remember not the former things, nor consider the things of old. Behold I am doing a new thing. Now it springs forth and you do not perceive it.' Don't worry about the things of old, Travis. You just keep looking out for the new thing and you'll be all right. I promise."

Travis nodded and then said, "Yeah. Okay. It's just that you talk about all the places that you've been and the wonders you've seen, and all I can remember is my mom and the trailer park. And Zion's Freedom. I'll never forget this place." Travis wiped his face and smiled.

"Now," DK said, "Why don't you show me again how well you shoot that rifle."

Just then a gray minivan rolled up behind them, trailing a cloud of dust. The van stopped abruptly and, after the engine was shut off, two doughy middle-aged men clambered out of the vehicle. They wore jeans and bright teal and purple windbreakers. "DK!" the driver of the minivan shouted. "DK, we need to talk to you."

The Reverend and Travis turned away from the target range to face them, Travis still holding the rifle. "Eric. Karl," DK stood and acknowledged the two men. "What can I do for you boys?"

"We thought you should know that our mother died last night," Eric, the driver of the van, said as he closed his door and stalked around the front of the vehicle towards DK.

DK nodded and said, "Thank you, boys. It's good of you to come all the way out here to let me know of your mother's passing. Your mother was a strong and decent woman. Always caring and always welcoming to anyone and everyone. I know you boys must miss her sorely, and she'll certainly be missed by the folks around here. They loved her."

Karl slammed his door shut as well and pointed his finger toward DK. "I've told you before about calling us boys. I'm not going to tell you again. I'm thirty-five years old, dammit! I'm not a boy. You stole our daddy's church and you seduced our mother to do it."

"Stole?" DK objected. "I've never stolen anything. Not from you. Not from anyone."

"You know that our daddy started this congregation. It should have passed to us when he died," Karl shouted. "What you did, the way you did it. The way you treated our mother . . . "

"What?" DK challenged them. "What do you want to say?"

"It was shameful, and it was wrong, and you know it."

The Reverend took a couple of steps toward the pair of men. "Now you boys know what the scriptures say. You know it says, 'Touch not the Lord's anointed and do my prophets no harm.' I'm pointing at you with my finger. Just my little finger for now. But if you come back here again, I will point at you with the finger of the Lord. And you boys know your scriptures well enough to know what happens to those who get the finger of the Lord pointed at them."

"We aren't scared of you, DK. You're a fraud and a cheat. A liar and a thief. You stole our daddy's church and you know it. You're a grifter. A swindler. You're nothing but a con man who's brainwashed these good people into following you."

"You should be afraid, boys," DK told them, his voice low. "You don't know the half of what I've done. And you surely don't know what I can do if I take the mind to do it. And I won't begin to describe the holy hell that these followers of mine will unleash if I ask them. Because they follow me, boys. And you don't want to get in the way of that."

It was then that Travis raised the AK-47 that he held and aimed it at the minivan. He fired round after round, shooting out the windows of the van. Glass shards flew in all directions. The two interlopers screamed and covered their heads as they dove for cover behind the van.

"Are you afraid now, boys?" DK shouted at them when Travis finished shooting out the windows and lowered the rifle. "Are you scared now?" DK laughed. "Your father, the late Reverend Zirkle, God bless him, may have started this congregation, but before he died he passed his prophetic mantle to me just like Elijah passed it to Elisha. And like Elisha to his mentor, Elijah, I'm twice the prophet your father was. And your mother knew it. She knew even then who I was destined to become. Now, you should know that I'm not angry with you boys because the prophet, the true prophet, is honored to be mocked and challenged. He has a feeling, an intuitive appreciation of these things. But you boys just don't seem to understand that. Now I'm sorry if you feel slighted. I'm sorry that you feel like you didn't get something that you were owed. I'm sorry you feel like you were passed over. But the leadership of this church was given to me by your father and not to either one of you. So what you need to do now is to go on and get back in your little van and get out of here because if you come back again, I'll have you arrested for trespassing."

"Our mother . . . " Eric began, but DK cut him off.

"Your mother was a beautiful, saintly woman and you boys never knew how to appreciate her until it was too late. If you had known her the way that I knew her, if you'd loved her the way that I loved her . . . "

"If we loved . . ." Karl stammered. "Why you!"

"Careful, Karl," DK warned pointing back toward Travis who still held the automatic rifle on them. "Triple-T there's a crack shot with that gun. If I say the word, he'll cut you both down before you can take another breath."

The two furious Zirkle brothers flushed red with anger, but relented. A small crowd of the Zion's Freedom members had gathered, drawn by the sound of the gunfire and shattering glass. They watched as Eric and Karl took off their jackets and used them to quickly brush the shards of broken glass out of the seats, then got into the van and drove away.

The Reverend DK, seeing the observers that had gathered there, pointed to Travis and quoted from the Bible again, "In the book of Joshua we read, 'Each of you will put a thousand of the enemy to flight for the Lord your God fights for you just as he promised.'" The members of the church cheered and applauded as DK held Travis' arm aloft as a sign of victory. "They will wage war against the Lamb, but the Lamb will overcome."

The members of the congregation shouted "Alleluia" and "Amen," and they cheered again for Travis and their leader because they'd fought off the enemy. They gathered around their leader and his young protégé and hugged them in celebration.

* * *

[From a transcript of a cassette tape recording of Reverend DK sermon—June 1992]

[Reverend DK] I remember Masada under the light of the full Israeli sun. I remember making the long trek up the serpentine path to reach that cliff top fortress where we died. If you go there today you take a cable car to the top. That makes it easier for tourists, I suppose. But when I was there— when I was there the first time in the year AD 73—we had to hike up and down that long and winding footpath any time that we needed anything. All our supplies had to be hauled up that slope. Looking east, we could see the briny Dead Sea and Jordan on the other side. We could smell the scent of salt blowing up from the Dead Sea. To the west was the Judean wilderness. Above us, I remember seeing a great many circling vultures. They knew death was coming to that place and they gathered in preparation for the feast.

I remember how the Roman army encamped below us. We could hear their officers shouting orders, even as far above them as we were. We watched them erecting their siege works and building their walls and the ramp they used to get up the western slope of the cliff. During the days they fired ballista bolts and stones into our camp. And at night we could see their campfires and hear the soldiers' drinking songs. And we all knew that this was the end. We knew that we were trapped there. We knew that we would die there, but we would not be turned out no matter what might happen to us.

We had hoped that if we could just hold out for long enough, then loyal Jews from across the land would come to our rescue. Even after the destruction of Jerusalem and the Holy Temple three years earlier, we still hoped. Hope lingers on. Even after the fire, there is hope. We clung to the hope that we had not been abandoned by God and that our brothers and sisters would rise up and come to our aid. We still believed that it would be possible to throw off the yoke of the Roman Empire. Or maybe we just hoped that it could still be possible.

We were freedom fighters. We were rebels, I suppose. We were rebels who refused to submit to the tyranny of Roman hegemony. But more than that, we were faithful. We were pure. We would not be corrupted by their unbelief. And, even if we died, even if we were killed, we trusted that, like the body of the Lord's anointed, our bodies would not see corruption. We were martyrs and we would be legends.

We were resolved that we would never be servants to Rome, or to any-one except God who alone is true and just. God alone is the Lord of mankind and we would serve no one else. We were the first to fight against the Romans and we pledged to fight to the very last against them. We wanted to live free—free to worship our God the way that our ancestors worshiped. But if we could not live free, we would do all that was in our power to die bravely and in a state of freedom.

When I went back to Masada several years ago in this life, as a young man, I saw something new, something that I hadn't seen when I was there before. I had a divine visitation in which I saw the angels of God. I saw the cherubim and the seraphim around the throne of God. I was shown all the things that pertain to the Law of God. I saw the coming of the Kingdom of Heaven. I saw the Lamb of God and I read from the scroll he held in his hand. That's where I had my first revelation. That's where I first began to understand who and what I am. I baptized myself in the Dead Sea as soon as I got back down to the bottom of the mountain—not an easy task, I assure you. Getting myself submerged in those salty waters was tricky because everything floats in the Dead Sea. But somehow I did it.

Now here, today, with you, I remember my experience at Masada. I remember it exactly. The past teaches us about the present and the present prepares us for the future. That's why we've gathered here at Zion's Freedom, to prepare ourselves for the future. to prepare ourselves for what is coming. The future follows from the past. Both proceed from the eternal present. And that's why we're here—To prepare ourselves for the future.

We are here to prepare ourselves for the end. Physically, mentally, spiritually, our whole spirit, soul, and body, preserved blameless unto the coming of our Lord Jesus Christ. We know that the end is coming. And we know that the end is coming soon. But we will be ready. Right?

[Cheers and shouts from the congregation]

[Reverend DK] What's that? We will be ready, right? We will be prepared for them no matter what hell they throw up against us. We are not Presbyterians or librarians. We are the community of God, strong and brave. We will be true to God and we will resist.

As it was written about me in the Dead Sea Scrolls—which were found not far from that Masada fortress, "the heavens and the earth will listen to obey his messiah." You have listened, and you have heard. Now you are prepared to obey. Yes? Yes?

[More cheers and applause from the congregation]

[End transcript]

Chapter Five

"I KNOW IT'S DIFFICULT, so I thank you for being so open and honest with me about all of this," Myron says. "Maybe you won't want to talk about some of this but I have to ask. It's an important part of the story. We need to talk about some of the allegations that were being made against the Reverend DK even before the confrontation at the compound and the tragic fire. We need to talk about the death of Marla Glenn."

"Go ahead," I tell him. "I'll answer if I can." I knew that Myron would ask about her eventually. Reporters always do. And I told him that I would tell him everything that I know. I'm not upset with Myron. I know that he's just trying to do his job.

"Your Reverend DK was wanted in connection to a murder, under the name of Lewis Earl Howard, right?"

"I don't know how much I can tell you about that. I never knew him by that name."

"You are aware by now that your Reverend DK, sometimes known by the name Sixten Johnson, used a number aliases, right?"

"Yeah. I guess I knew something about that."

"He had a number of aliases and false names that he used in different situations. He sometimes used the aliases Timothy Tuttle and Daryl Bridges. He also used the name Lewis Earl Howard. He was wanted under that name by the police in connection to a murder in Zionsville, Indiana—about twenty miles northeast of Indianapolis—in 1982, when he was twenty-three years old."

"I don't know very much about that," I tell Myron. I'm aware that DK used other names, but I only ever knew him as DK. And Sixten, I guess.

"Well, just tell me what you know. Tell me what you can."

"DK told us only a little bit about that when the investigators showed up. He said it was a case of misunderstanding. A deliberate misunderstanding, he said. And that he was innocent of the accusations the police made." I tell this to Myron, but I can't help to chuckle a little as I finish.

"What's funny?" he asks.

"Zionsville. Seems funny."

"Yeah. He was in trouble in Zionsville when he was a young man, and he died in Zion's Freedom. It's another of those funny coincidences that make life seem so weird."

I tell Myron again, "I don't know anything more about it. Really." I can feel him staring at me from the dark.

"Her name was Marla Glenn. She was sixteen years old when he got her pregnant. He was twenty-two. That was in 1981. Seven years later he showed up in Arizona with a different name and almost immediately began maneuvering to take over Zion's Freedom from the Zirkles."

"I've heard people talk about this Marla Glenn woman, but I don't know anything about her. DK never talked to us about her."

"She turned up dead, along with the baby. She was strangled to death, and the baby in her belly died with her. And coincidentally—maybe—he went missing at that same time."

"She was pregnant? I hadn't heard that."

"The coroner's report indicates that she was three months pregnant when she was strangled to death."

I don't know what I should say. So I tell Myron exactly that. "I don't know what I should say." He says that it's okay and that we can talk about something else.

✳ ✳ ✳

[From a transcript of a cassette tape recording of Revered DK sermon—June 1992]

[Reverend DK] The world is going through its final death throes. If you listen you can hear the wheeze of its final breath. You can hear the death rattle of the world. The end isn't near—the end is here. Darkness is coming for the world and it's the darkness of the grave. The moon will be turned to blood and the sun will be dimmed. The stars will forbear to shine. Darkness. Full dark.

But this darkness isn't for us. We live in the light.

Your children won't have to grow up. The littlest ones among us will never know the hardship of getting old. They won't have arthritis or

Alzheimer's. They won't need dentures in their mouths or bifocal lenses for their eyes because we don't have that long until the end. The darkness is here. We have at most five years before the end of the world. But darkness is not the end. And death is not the end. There is darkness and there is light. There is death and there is life. Rebirth. There is light after dark. There is new life after old death.

And the book of Revelation—I want you to note this, by the way. It is the book of Revelation -singular. Not Revelations—plural. I hate when people call it Revelations. Especially ministers. They should know better. Whenever I hear someone say Revelations, I know that they don't know how to rightly divide the word of God. Don't trust anyone who says Revelations.

Anyway, the book of Revelation is the key to understanding all of this. It is the key to understanding everything. If you want to know what is going to happen in the future, if you want to understand what is happening now, you have to open the seven seals. It's an apocalyptic drama with tragedy, and horror, and not a little comedy thrown in, but those seals must be opened. And I am opening and interpreting those seals for you.

And what happens when the seventh seal is broken? What happens when the Lamb of God opens the seventh seal? Can anyone tell me?

[Muttering among the congregation]

[Reverend DK] Louisa? What happens when the seventh seal is opened?

[Louisa Mendez] There's silence in heaven, DK.

[Reverend DK] Silence in heaven. That's right. There's silence in heaven for about half an hour. And what have I told you about silence?

[Muttering from the congregation]

[Reverend DK] That silence is me. That's me. I am the silence of God. And if I am mentioned in the book of Revelation, do you think it possible that maybe you are as well? Well it's true. You are. You're all there with me.

[Shouts of affirmation and joy from the congregation]

[Reverend DK] What does it say in Revelation chapter four? Can anyone tell me? Anyone? No? Well I'll tell you. Revelation chapter four describes the throne room of heaven and how the one true God is seated there on his throne, surrounded by the thrones of the twenty-four elders. And round about the throne were four and twenty seats, and upon the seats I saw four and twenty elders sitting, clothed in white raiment, and they had on their heads crowns of gold. And the four and twenty elders fall down before him that sat on the throne, and worship him that liveth for ever and ever, and cast their crowns before the throne saying, "Thou art worthy, o Lord, to receive glory, and honor, and power, for thou hast created all things, and for thy pleasure they are and were created." Now—how many of you are there here with us at Zion's Freedom?

[Muttering from the congregation]

[Reverend DK] There were, get this, there were twenty-four elders sitting on twenty-four thrones surrounding the one throne of the One who rules in heaven. And just how many of you are there here with me tonight? Miss Louisa, will you stand up and count heads real quick?

[Louisa Mendez counting]

[Louisa Mendez] There are twenty-four of us here with you, Reverend DK.

[Reverend DK] There are twenty-four of you. That's right, Louisa. Thank you. Absolutely right. Twenty-four. This is not an accident. And this is no coincidence. This is the grand design of God written before the creation of the world. You, Melvin Schaeffer, Giselle [Jacobson], you Marie [Mason], all of you here tonight, you are part of the grand design of God for the end times and the end of the world. We may not be mighty in number, but we are part of something bigger than ourselves. We are part of the grand design of God.

I've talked with some of you about this before. Others of you are hearing it for the first time. That's okay. We're all learning together. Some of you have told me that you don't feel old enough to be considered an 'elder,' and I understand that. I'm looking at you Giselle [Jacobson]. You can't be a day older than thirty-three. Am I right?

[Giselle Jacobson] Oh, DK. You charmer. . .

[Laughter from the congregation]

[Reverend DK] Seriously though. This being an elder around the throne of God is not about your age. It's about the time you've spent in the true understanding. This experience that you are having with me now, and with each other here tonight, is preparing you to be those elders. God is making you more than you are. God is making all of us more than we are. This is his grand design.

[End transcript]

✶ ✶ ✶

"I'm sorry to keep coming back to this, Travis. I know that it's difficult for you to discus these things, even after all these years. But I need to ask a few more questions on this topic."

I nod and let Myron know that it's okay. That I'm still willing to answer his questions if I can.

"Two agents from the Federal Bureau of Investigation came out to the compound to interview the Reverend DK—agents Marcus and Ramirez. Were you there when they questioned him about his relationship with Marla Glenn?"

"No. I only saw them as they were leaving."

"What happened?"

"I'd been out with Tim and Aaron. Their moms didn't let them come visit me at the compound very often. I think this was the last time I saw them."

"What did you boys do?"

"They brought beer and cigarettes, like before. But I told them that I really didn't do those things anymore. The beer might have been okay, but I was definitely done with cigarettes. Instead we took the ATVs out and rode around for a couple of hours. We got back to the compound just as the agents were leaving in their car."

"So you didn't hear anything of their conversation with DK?"

"No. But he told me about it and I could tell that he was really upset."

"What, if anything, did DK tell you about his conversation with the agents?"

"Not much, except that he was distressed and that he hadn't known that she'd been pregnant."

"I thought you said that you didn't know about the pregnancy," Myron says but I don't respond. "Well, what do you think he meant?"

"I shift on the stool where I'm sitting. I've been here a long time and I'm starting to get uncomfortable. I need to pee, but I'm reluctant to stop the interview. I promised that I would do it and I will. "I don't know. But he was very sad. He said that he'd made a mistake."

"What mistake was that? Do you think that he killed her? Do you think that's what he meant?"

"That's what everyone says, right? that he killed her. . ."

"But do *you* think that he killed her, Travis?"

I do not answer for a long time. "I don't know. And since he's dead now, I guess we'll never know."

CHAPTER FIVE

* * *

Behind the garage where the members of Zion's Freedom parked their vehicles, two towering Ponderosa pines created a hidden bit of shade where Travis liked to sit when he wanted to be alone. He didn't come to this spot often as he enjoyed the company of his new family and friends at the compound and wanted to be with them. But there were times when a boy wanted—needed—a moment to himself, away from the eyes of the others.

DK found Travis there with red, puffy eyes. He'd been crying. "Travis, tell me what's going on," he said gently.

"Nothing." Travis sniffed and wiped his nose. "I'm fine."

"I know," DK said. "I know. But still. You should tell me."

Travis looked up and said, "I don't know what it is. I think I just miss my mom."

"I'm sure you do. Would be surprised if you didn't."

"I just didn't want you to think that I wasn't happy here, or anything."

DK motioned for Travis to follow him and the two of them climbed on DK's motorcycle. They made a quick stop at the grocery store to purchase a bouquet of cut flowers—white and red carnations—and drove out to Fairview Cemetery where the two of them stood quietly at Brenda's grave. "We put up some money for the headstone," DK explained. "We never got to know your mom, but we wanted to do this for you. It was our gift."

"Oh. Thanks." Several silent minutes passed and then Travis knelt down and laid the flowers across the headstone. "Thanks," he said again.

"Do you want to say anything to her?" DK prompted.

"No. I don't think so. It's just good to know she's here. That she's okay."

DK nodded and allowed Travis a few more minutes of silence. When Travis indicated that he was done, DK said, "Would you like to see some interesting headstones? I've been out here many times—it's one of my favorite places—and I've found some curious headstones. They're worth checking out.

"Sure," Travis said and DK lead the boy to a small, rounded stone covered with lichen that was inscribed with the words:

Here lies Juliet, the willing BRIDE
Twice married, but a virgin when she DIED

"It sounds like a joke right?" Travis said, chuckling and wiping away the last of the tears in his eyes. "But it's not, is it? It can't be, can it?"

"Exactly. But, I mean, here it is," DK said. "It's carved in her headstone for all eternity. Or for at least as long as these stones endure. Even stones aren't forever."

They walked to another part of the cemetery and found another grave marker—a tall, smooth monolith with the inscription:

Simon Gilker—Died July 4, 1896—Age 48
Killed by means of a Rocket

"Think about it for a bit," DK said. "You'll understand why I think it's amusing."

After a few seconds Travis laughed. "Oh man . . . Killed by a rocket on July fourth. That's too crazy."

"Yeah, crazy it is." DK grinned. "I've got one more for you to see." They strolled a few feet further to a spot near one of the Mediterranean Cyprus trees that ornamented the grounds.

Here lies David Haas
August 7, 1805—September 30, 1838
Had both of his legs severed from his body
by a cannonball. He endured with great fortitude
but died, in the end, from a loss of blod.

"Blod?" Travis asked.

"I'm sure it should be 'blood.' Such a tragic story. Such a terrible place for a spelling error."

"Well," Travis said with a creeping grin. "At least it won't be there forever." DK mussed his hair and the two of them walked back to the motorcycle.

* * *

[From a transcript of a cassette tape recording of Reverend DK sermon—June 1992]

[Reverend DK] Take a look at Moses. Look what happened to him and think about it. He was run out of Egypt for a misunderstanding. A misunderstanding that looked like murder. But it wasn't. It wasn't murder. But he went into hiding in the wilderness of Midian just the same. He assumed the identity of a shepherd in Midian for forty years. He had to flee from his home in Egypt—he'd grown up in the house of the Pharaoh, raised as the grandson of the Pharaoh, the adopted son of Pharaoh's daughter—but he was forced to flee into the wilderness. Even though he was completely innocent, he had to run for his very life.

And Moses, hiding in Midian, met up with Jethro, who was a priest of Midian. Now sometimes Jethro's called Jethro, and other times he's called Reuel and sometimes he's called Raguel, and sometimes he's called Hobab. This man had almost as many names as the phone book. And this Jethro with the many names was a Kenite shepherd, but he was also a priest of the Lord. Now the question I want to ask you is this: How did this gentile shepherd living out in the wilderness and desert of Midian come to be a priest of the Living God? Who trained him? He was a priest even before the priesthood was established with Moses' brother Aaron. So how exactly did he come to have a religious community to lead in the wilderness? How was it established?

[Sudden murmur of conversation and gasps from the congregation]

[Reverend DK] Well, would you look at that? It's a praying mantis. Do you see it? He just flew in through the window and landed on my shoulder. He's a big one, isn't he? What is that—three inches long? He's huge. Wow. Just look at those wings. Beautiful.

[Excited noises from the congregation]

[Reverend DK] Hey. Wow. Look at this, everyone. This is an auspicious sign. Doubly so, really. It's a praying mantis, of course, which should say something to us about the importance of prayer. This beautiful insect is a sign that we should pray. But even more than that, it's important to note that the word "mantis" comes to us from a Greek word that means "soothsayer" or "prophet." Now you already know that I am the prophet of the Lord. I've told you this and demonstrated it with signs. But if you didn't already believe me, this should be your sign. This is a sign for you to believe. Gideon, do you believe that I am the prophet of the Lord?

[Gideon Lamont] I do, Reverend.

[Reverend DK] John. John Hawkins. Do you believe that I am the prophet of the Lord?

[John Hawkins] Yes, DK. I believe.

[Reverend DK] What about you, Josh? Do you believe?

[Josh Zamecnik] I do. I believe. You are the prophet.

[Reverend DK] And what do you believe, Mr. Zamecnik? What does it mean to you that I am the prophet of the Lord?

[Josh Zamecnik] Nothing the prophet does is wrong. Nothing the prophet does *can* be wrong. That's why you were chosen to be the prophet, DK. And we pray every day for our prophet. We pray that he will be true.

[Reverend DK] That's good, Josh. That's good. But let's get back to the question we had before the prophetic mantis swooped down to give us our sign: How is the priesthood of God established outside the normal bounds of the religious community? God declares it so. That's it. God declares it and it is. No other mechanism. No other requirement. God declared Jethro, who was Reuel, and Raguel, and Hobab to be the priest of Midian, and he was the priest of Midian. God declared it. That's all that was necessary. He didn't need accreditation from anyone. He didn't need their validation. God declared him to be a priest and that was it. He was a priest of the Lord because God said he was.

And there he goes, folks. Our little visitor has, with his message delivered, flown away into the night. I think we should pray now.

[End transcript]

*　*　*

"Do you still believe in DK and what he taught during his time at the Zion's Freedom compound? It's been thirty years and, despite all that's happened, you've never said anything against him—not publicly anyway. Do you still believe in him? That he was a prophet from God?"

It takes me a long time to answer because I haven't really considered what I believe about DK. And it's hard to believe that it's been such a long time since all of it happened. Has it really been thirty years? "DK never lied to me," I tell Myron after a few seconds. "That's all I know. He never lied to me."

"Do you still believe he was the prophet?"

"Like I said, he never lied to me. That's all I know."

"That's fine, Travis. That's fine. Let me ask you about something else."

"Okay."

"Tell me about Cornelius Howard."

But I don't recognize that name. "Who?"

"Cornelius Howard. He went by the nickname Hobart, I believe."

Now I remember. "Hobart! Yeah, I remember him," I say.

"He's the only member of your community to leave voluntarily."

"The only one?" I hadn't really thought about it, but it sounds about right, I suppose. Folks were loyal to DK. No one wanted to leave.

"He called his sister in Yuma from a pay phone at the SuperSuds laundry-mat in Superior. He told her that he was coming home, but he never arrived. She called the police to report him missing the next morning, but they never found him. In fact, he's still missing, thirty years later."

I did not know abut that. "Where did he go?"

"That's a very good question, Travis," Myron says gently. "A very good question. We were hoping that you might be able to help us find him."

* * *

The room was hot and the air was dead. Motionless and stale. The window AC unit chugged along as well as it could, but it did little to bring down the temperature of the room. The members of Zion's Freedom were gathered together in that stuffy room for Bible study—men, women, and children. The whole sweating congregation. And they'd been there since just after dinner. As soon as the tables were cleared and the dishes were washed and dried, they assembled together in the Bible study hall. It was now going on 11:30 and the Reverend DK was still shouting at them about the proper method of biblical exegesis.

"The Bible is the word of God, yes?" He paused for a response from his followers. When they didn't respond immediately, he prompted them sharply. "The Bible is the word of God, yes? Let me hear you."

"Yes," they answered back dully.

"And the Bible is true and accurate and provides everything we need to live holy and productive lives in this world, yes?"

"Yes," they answered again, trying to get back into the call and response rhythm.

"Right," DK said. "But what you gotta' understand is that this Bible here, it's not the whole story. What we've got here—and there's a lot here. Look at all these pages," he said fanning out the pages of his large Bible. "Look at all this material, from Genesis to Revelation—what we've got here is just the surface level. There's so much more. What we've got here is like the headlines on a newspaper. You get some information in the headlines, enough to have an idea of what's going on in the world. But there's so much more information in the article that follows the headline. You've gotta' read the whole story. And what we've got here in the Bible, while it's true and accurate and useful to our lives, it's not enough. You need the rest of the story. And that's why I'm here. That's why you've come to me. I'm trying to tell you the rest of the story."

Little Luke Matthews, eight years old, the eldest son of Marsha and Gary Matthews, sat next to his 'uncle Hobart.' But it was late and he was young. Luke's head bobbed forward and jerked back again as he struggled to stay awake. Cornelius Howard patted him on the back and rubbed his shoulders. "Be strong, little buddy," he said to the boy. "Be strong."

"I'm tired, Uncle Hobart," little Luke said. And he looked it. The poor boy had done lessons with the home school group all morning, then worked in the vegetable gardens after lunch. And now he'd sat through five and a half hours of the Reverend DK's lecturing about the differences between figurative and allegorical exegesis. He had nothing left in his young reserve.

Uncle Hobart raised his hand for permission to speak. "Can we take a short break, DK? Some of us need to use the restroom and the little ones should be getting to bed soon."

DK whirled around and glared at Cornelius Howard. "You want to take a break, do you? You want to let the little ones rest? Well, I'll tell you Hobart, the enemies of God are approaching. They're coming soon. They're coming for us. They're already on their way. And do you think they'll let you rest because you're tired and you need to relieve your bladder? You need to toughen up. You all need to toughen up," he said to the whole room.

"But, DK. . ." Hobart tried again.

"Are you questioning me?" DK railed. "Are you questioning me?'

"No," Hobart said quietly. "Except that it is late and this has been going on for too long already. You are our prophet and we'll follow you, but we're human and we need to rest. We can't give no more."

Other members of the congregation nodded their affirmation of this. Others, who were less bold, kept their faces stony, giving away nothing of their inner struggles.

"No. We're going to continue until I'm done." DK spat the words.

"DK, please. Listen to reason. You're asking too much."

Now DK was furious. He closed his Bible and thumped it down on the lectern at which he was standing. "Too much? You think that I'm demand-ing too much of you?"

Hobart glanced around the room trying to gauge his support in the room, but even those who'd nodded their assent to his words before were now mute and poker faced. Dead eyed and silent as stones. He turned back to DK. "I know I'm not alone when I say it DK, even if the others are too scared of you to admit it right now, but you ask too much. And it's not just tonight."

"Tell me more about this," DK said. His voice was calm and measured but his body was tense and rigid.

"You ask too much. You control how we're dressed and what we wear. You monitor what time we go to bed at night and what time we get up in the morning. You approve what books we can read. We have to sign in and out of the compound—out of Zion's *Freedom* compound—like prisoners. You ask too much."

"Are you saying that you feel like a prisoner here? Do you think I'm being tyrannical?"

"I'm just saying that you ask too much," Hobart said weakly.

"Well, I wouldn't want anyone to feel like a prisoner here in their home. This is a place of freedom, so anyone who wants to leave with Mister Howard is free to go."

"DK," Hobart objected. "I don't want to leave. I just want. . . "

"What?" DK demanded. "What is it you want?"

"DK. . ." Hobart pleaded, but DK said nothing. "Fine. Fine. I'll leave in the morning."

"No," DK roared. "You'll leave tonight. You'll leave now, this very moment."

"Now? Right now? Tonight?"

"Yes," said DK. "You'll leave tonight. I don't want anyone to think I'm keeping you here against your will. Don't bother to gather up your stuff. Just get out."

* * *

"And that was the last you saw of Cornelius Howard, the last you saw of Hobart?"

"It was. I never saw him again," I say. To be honest, I hadn't thought about him much either."

"No one ever saw him again, apparently," Myron says.

"What do you think happened to him?" I ask.

"I don't know," Myron tells me. "The general consensus is that he's probably dead, but no one knows for certain."

"Oh" I don't know what else to say. I liked Uncle Hobart until he left."

"Were the members of Zion's Freedom allowed to leave?" Myron asks me.

"Yeah, I guess so. But I don't think many did. Only Uncle Hobart while I was there. I think maybe they were afraid to leave." I stop because that's not quite right. "Not afraid to leave, but afraid of what was outside. They were terrified beyond the gates, because outside the church they weren't safe."

"Tell me something about these marathon Bible study sessions," Myron says after a moment of silence. "How often did you have sessions like this? Sessions that went on for hours on end?"

"At first it wasn't every night. At first it was just the regular Wednesday night Bible studies. But later it got to be most every night. Especially toward the end."

"And how long did these sessions last?"

"Oh, he'd go on till at least 10 or 10:30 most nights. Sometimes later. I didn't understand most of what he said, but I did like listening to him. He could really talk."

"Was he taking amphetamines, perhaps?"

"What?"

"Was he taking some sort of amphetamine? Or cocaine maybe? Was he taking something for the energy to keep up with all those endless hours of lecturing?"

"No," I tell him. "No. No. At least I don't think so."

Chapter Six

Breakfast the next morning was scrambled egg collected from the chickens kept on the compound and fried mushrooms served with buttered toast and biscuits and gallons of whole milk and hot coffee to wash it down—all prepared for the group by Maggie Snow and Opal Mills - two women of the group who enjoyed cooking for everyone. All the women took turns cooking meals in rotation. The Zion's Freedom family enjoyed the meals prepared by Maggie. The meals prepared by Joan Ahntholz, not so much. No one except her husband, Carter, had anything good to say about the meals she prepared. But everyone pitched in around the compound. Everyone did their share around the camp. Some repaired car engines. Some took care of the animals. Some worked in the gardens. Everyone worked and everyone ate and there were few complaints - even about Joan's cooking.

That morning, as his followers were consuming their morning repast, with the golden light of the sun filtering in through the eastern windows of the refectory, Reverend DK addressed the group. "If you love God," he said gently, without any of the shouting he'd employed the night before during the Bible study, "then you must love me. It comes down to that. If you love God, then you have to love me. You have to love and adore me, worship me almost. It's that important. I don't want to sound harsh and I don't want to be cruel. And if it sounded that way last night, I am sorry. I apologize. But it's simply this: what is written in this book is written of me. It's a revelation of Jesus Christ and it's a revelation of me. That's why I'm so hard on some of you. that's why I have to be so firm. I can't be easy on you. These are hard times and we live hard lives."

"Listen, I have no defensiveness about any of this. I am not trying to hide anything from you. I am just as you see me, just as God made me. And without me it will be nothing but darkness, and futile desires for you. It will be nothing but ignorance, and fatal jealousies. Is that the future that you want to see? Is that the path you want to go down?"

The congregation continued their meal in silent surrender. Some nodded but no one said anything. The only sound was that of forks scraping on plates and the occasional sip of coffee.

"I didn't sleep last night," DK continued, "because the Lord kept showing me, over and over, that our friend, our so-called friend, Hobart's position among the priesthood is now in question. Like it says in the scriptures, 'They went out from us, but they were not of us; for if they had been of us, they would no doubt have continued with us. But they went out, that they might be made manifest that they were not all of us.' Cornelius Howard is no longer among us. He's gone out from us. And he's joined the enemy. He's joined the angels of darkness and all the sons of perdition. Perhaps he can be saved even yet. I don't know. Perhaps we can save him, but it's doubtful. Once someone goes over to the other side, it's incredibly difficult to bring them back. But ye," DK said continuing, "ye have an unction from the Holy One, and ye know all things. You know the truth here. A man may be mocked by truth, but you now the truth here."

He paused again, deep in thought. The members of the community continued eating in silence. Then he spoke again. "Carol, I want you to bring those pictures that you showed me earlier. Bring me those photos. Bring them here for everyone to see."

Carol Hendrickson, who had been pushing the last couple of bites of eggs around on her plate, nodded and jumped up to find the scrapbook of photos she kept for the community. She returned in a rush with the photos of Cornelius and handed them to DK. He thumbed through them, glancing briefly at each one. Photos of Cornelius riding in the community's little pickup truck, smiling at an amusing thought, of Cornelius holding up a line of small mouth bass he'd caught on a fishing trip with the men from the group, of Cornelius dressed in his Sunday suit, standing awkwardly at the pulpit in front of the congregation. The photos showed him as a happy member of the family.

"Burn all his pictures," DK announced to the group as he tossed the photos on the table. "Burn them. He went out from among us, he left us. So do not think of him anymore. Do not consider him. Burn his pictures. If you have any correspondence from him, any letters or notes, burn those as well. By his own choice he has gone out from us, so let him be gone from our minds."

The room was silent until DK continued. "It must be the priesthood of God or nothing! Nothing else. Do you understand me? The lifestyle of angels demands perfection. And we are alone in the world—a world that is already in flames. The world is inflamed. It is us against the forces of Babylon. And the business of Babylon is our death. The business of Babylon is our destruction."

* * *

[From a transcript of a cassette tape recording of Bible study session— July 1992]

[Reverend DK] Emmett, stand up there and say a few words for us. Tell everyone how you came to be here.

[Emmett Fischer] I praise God and give glory to his servant, DK, because I am grateful to be here tonight. I know how close I came to not being here at all.

[Murmur from the congregation]

[Emmett Fischer] It was a little over a year ago that I first met our good Reverend DK. I think he saved my life. This was just after my wife left me. She just walked out on me on New Year's Day. Told me that we were done and she walked out. And I wasn't handling it well. I got really drunk. I drank almost an entire bottle of Maker's Mark whiskey. And, like I said, I was really drunk, right? And that's when I got it in my head that I needed something to eat, you know, so I wouldn't be so drunk, right? So I walked across four lanes of highway traffic to the gas station where I could get a couple of slices of pizza. Four lanes—drunk as a dog. I don't know how I did it, but I got across those four lanes of highway and I got my pizza. And I ate it right there in the parking lot of the gas station. And when I was done I started back across those same four lanes of highway traffic, still drunk. To this day, I don't know how I did it. And I did it twice, back and forth. Anyway, DK was there on the other side, waiting for me, I think. He told me that he saw me staggering and he knew that I needed help. And, God bless him, he was right. He helped me find some peace. And he kept me from making another trip out across the highway that night. And, praise God, he got me off the whiskey.

[Appreciative murmurs from the congregation]

[Emmett Fischer] God bless you, Reverend DK. And may God bless Zion's Freedom.

[Reverend DK] Thank you, Emmett. Thank you. Now does anyone else have a word of testimony? What about you Goyathlay? What's the word from our token foreign missionary?

[Goyathlay Hernandez] *Gracias a Dios y gracias a su siervo. Dios bendiga su silencio.*

[Applause from the congregation]

[Reverend DK] Folks, folks. Listen. Goyathlay here is a miracle from God. Born the son of a Native American mother and a Mexican father, he was homeless when I first met him. He was panhandling off the Maricopa Freeway. He's a good man. Faithful and true, like the best of God's servants.

[Goyathlay Hernandez] *Gracias, señor. Gracias, DK.*

[End transcript]

* * *

"Tell me about your relationship with DK," Myron says.

"What do you mean?"

"You were, what? Fourteen years old when you met him, and he was already in his thirties. . . "

"So?" I'm not sure what Myron is driving at.

"Some have speculated that he. . . "

I understand now. "You think that he what? Took advantage of me? That he was some sort of kiddie diddler?"

"Well . . . ," Myron hesitates.

"No. He wasn't Not at all. He never touched me like that. And I get damned tired of people sayin' that he might of. DK never did anything but be nice to me."

"I'm sorry, Travis. I'm sorry to have cast aspersions on your friend."

"Aspersions?"

"I'm sorry to have said something that might have been construed as slanderous. That was not my intent. I want to understand what happened at Zion's Freedom—that's what this documentary project is all about—and I won't be able to do that if I am bringing rumor and innuendo into the story instead of waiting to hear the truth. I offer you my sincere apology, Travis. I am sorry."

"Well, I don't know about innuendo," I tell him. "But DK was always good to me. I never had a father and he was, for the time that I was there, what I'd always imagined a father would be like. He took me for rides through the mountains on his motorcycle. He showed me how to fix a carburetor on the bike. He shared good music with me. He was my friend. I never had a dad, but if I did, I would of wanted him to be like DK."

* * *

The two of them were covered in sweat and grease. DK's little motorcycle was parked and disassembled over a plastic tarpaulin. Each part was arranged in neat rows on the blue plastic sheet. "Now that we've removed the carburetor we need to clean all of its various components. We'll scrub them with a cleaning solution and a stiff brush to remove the dirt and grease and grime." DK handed Travis a nylon brush and said, "Let's start scrubbing."

For the next hour they scoured and scrubbed the parts clean, then rinsed them in a bucket of clean water and laid them out to dry. "What we've got here, Triple-T, is our very own version of *Zen and the Art of Motorcycle Maintenance.*" DK chuckled. "Except I don't know all that much about Zen and cleaning the carburetor is about all I know how to do with the motorcycle maintenance."

"What's Zen?" Travis asked.

"Zen is a Japanese practice of meditation, a practice by which one can find wisdom and compassion by awakening one's inner nature. It begins with a denial of the self and the ego, and a recognition that desire is the source of all human suffering."

Travis stopped scrubbing and looked up. "What's that go to do with motorcycles?"

"I don't know, Triple-T," DK laughed. "I never actually read the book. I don't know. And I don't think anyone really knows." DK opened the plastic cooler they kept beside them as they worked and handed it to Travis. "Share a beer with me."

Travis wiped the grease from his hands with an old rag and sat down with the bottle from DK. He took a big swig and smiled with satisfaction. "How'd you learn to do all this?"

"I never had a dad around to teach me any of it," DK said. "I picked it up bit by bit, here and there, the same way I learned most of what I know about everything."

"Did you go to school?"

"Not as such. I mean, I did. But I don't have a degree or anything. I took classes at the University of Minnesota for a while—studied philosophy and literature, but I dropped out before I finished."

"School's dumb anyway," Travis said sullenly. He picked up a stone and tossed it into the distance.

"Well it is and it isn't," DK said. "For some it can open up a whole world of experiences. Books can do that for some. They can open up new worlds, strange and exciting worlds. Foreign worlds with marvelous adventures. But for others," he paused and took a long sip of his beer. "For others like you and me, well, we've just got to get out there and see the world. Right? We've got to get the motorcycle grease on our hands and the wind in our hair."

"Yeah," Travis smiled and the two of them stared at the desert vista spread out in front of them.

"South-east of here, down in Mexico, there's a cool place that I should show you sometime. It's called the Zone of Silence out in the Chuauahuahn desert. It's nothing but a flat and nasty stretch of empty desert with only mesquite and cactus to decorate the landscape. But there's something strange out there. Something inexplicable."

"What is it?" Travis asked.

"It's sorta' like the Bermuda Triangle, but in the desert instead of the ocean. No one really knows what it is. Or why. No one can explain it—but in this dismal patch of Mexican desert all radio signals inexplicably disappear. They just evaporate into static. Compasses spin like crazy. Planes and rockets flying through the region crash right down to the ground. Back in the 70s, the US Air Force lost one of their rockets there. It was carrying two containers full of radioactive Cobalt-57. So they sent out a team of investigators to find their missing rocket - including one Wernher von Braun, the Nazi scientist who helped develop the US space program after World War Two. They brought back hundreds of tons of soil and rock, thinking that there might be something in them to explain the strange effects of the area. Perhaps they thought they'd discover underground deposits of magnetite or debris from meteorites, or UFOs, or something. Who knows? But whatever it was that brought back with them, they still couldn't figure it out. Whatever it is that's out there remains beyond scientific explanation."

"That's so wild," Travis said. "Do you think we can go see it?"

"Well, we can't go anywhere at all until we get this bike fixed up," DK said pointing to all the parts laid out on the tarp. "Now that they're all dry we're going to reassemble the whole thing and mount it back in the engine. Hopefully we won't have any parts left over when we're done." The two of them laughed together at the familiar joke.

* * *

[From a transcript of a cassette tape recording of Bible session—July 1992]

[Reverend DK] Before we conclude for the night, does anyone have any questions? Anything they want to ask me? Yeah, Josh?

[Josh Zamecnik] Can you tell us something more about the forces of Babylon?

[Reverend DK] Yeah. Yeah, man. Yeah. You got to know that it's coming back, Babylon. And really, it never disappeared, did it? Just went into hiding for a while, biding its time. Waiting to have another chance on the world's stage. Now I've been following events in the news with this war in Iraq and I've heard how they're rebuilding the city of Babylon - I've seen the photos of the rebuilt Gates of Ishtar. Billions of dollars to do it, and much of it American money. But why go halfway around the world to visit the Antichrist's theme park in the desert when you could go on up to Washington DC. to see it just the same? You don't even need a passport for that. Babylon - Gogmagog - all the megalomania of evil you could stand to see is just the other side of this country of ours. It's the propaganda of any king, the towers built by Sargon the Great in Sumeria, built by Herod in Israel, built by Saddam the Mighty in Iraq, built by Donald J. Trump in New York City. . . It's all the same Babylon. Anyone else have any questions? Yes, Melvin?

[Melvin Schaeffer] With all that's happening in the world, all that's going wrong, what do we do about the radical, liberal Democrats in Washington that are. . .

[Reverend DK] Hold on. Hold on. Hold on. I'm going to stop you right there, Melvin. I'm going to stop you before you get to your question, okay. And I know it's rude to interrupt, so I'm sorry. But I've got to stop you before you go too far wrong here, okay?

[Melvin Schaeffer] Yes. Okay.

[Reverend DK] Because it's not really about the liberals in the government. And it's not about the conservatives, either. It's not about the left or the right. It's not about politics. It's not about Republican or Democrat. I mean—Ted Bundy was an active Republican. And John Wayne Gacy was an assistant precinct captain for a local Democratic Party candidate. What does it matter, Republican or Democrat? It doesn't matter at all. The whole system is heartless and immoral. The FBI is selling drugs and the CIA is assassinating elected officials in South America. It's open warfare by the government - from both sides, Republican and Democrat - for the heart and the mind and the soul of this country. It's not about this or that political party. Do you understand what I'm saying?

[Melvin Schaeffer] Yeah, I think so. Thank you, DK. Thank you.

[Reverend DK] Hear me on this. The American eagle is not a glorious, patriotic bird. The eagle will eat in three ways—like other predatory raptors, it will eat what it captures and kills. But the eagle is an opportunist that will also eat what it can steal from other birds and mammals. And, and, get this, they're also carrion eaters. They are scavengers that will eat rotting corpses. They will eat the putrid things they find decomposing on the ground. They're disgusting creatures. And this is exactly what the Gospel of Matthew tells us - "where the corpse is, there the eagles will gather." Do you see that? The eagle, the symbol of America, is a predatory, opportunist, carrion eater. It's not a liberal thing. It's not a conservative thing. But it is an authentically American thing.

Think about this. Consider it. We would celebrate the one who tried to plant a bomb in Adolf Hitler's briefcase. We'd call that man a hero. But we would scourge and condemn the man who tried to put a bomb on J. P. Morgan's doorstep. We'd condemn the man who tried to assassinate a famous capitalist, someone like Donald J. Trump. I'm just saying that it's not about the violence of the bomb or the gun. It's not the violence we object to. To resist fascist dictators with bombs and guns is laudable, but to resist the capitalists and plutocrats, and oligarchs with dynamite, or by any means really, is loathsome in American and is condemned by Republicans and Democrats alike.

Now they're rebuilding Babylon right in front of our eyes. Rome has returned. Babylon has returned. The future is not the future—it's the past re-imagined. If you wait around long enough everything comes back around. I've seen it before and you'll see it again. One of those science-fiction writers—I forget his name—says that we're living in a black iron prison that is imperial Rome of the distant past superimposed over the present time. He says it is the empire that never ended—full of artificial people and inauthentic humans—all of them slaves and victims. We feel the spaces of time and attempt to measure them—but it is all one. The future is the past re-imagined. Rewritten. The prophecies of scripture are accurate, not because the prophets could see future events, but because they were rewriting history. Genghis Khan, Napoleon, Woodrow Wilson, Julius Caesar—all of them will come again. And this is good news because Caesar still owes me twenty bucks.

[Laughter from the congregation]

[Reverend DK] Is there anything else? Does anyone else have a question that I can answer?

[Unidentified voice from the congregation] What can you tell us of the future?

[Reverend DK] How can I teach about the future? Or to say it another way, how can I give you present indications of future events? For what doesn't exist yet can't be taught. Right? Now, I'm not usually one to make prognostications about the future, but let me suggest a few things that I see on the horizon. Robots will, by the year 1996, be programmed to function as psychiatrists and be enabled to both give advice and prescribe medications. It's coming folks and it won't be long. Already they're developing the artificial intelligence that will be used to program these psychiatric robots. I can also say that the current war in Iraq will not be the last. We will win this war, and quickly, but we won't finish what we've started and we will be forced to return to Babylon.

And I think that will be all for tonight. Goodnight, everyone.

[End transcript]

* * *

DK sat on a three legged stool at the front of the auditorium style room with the members of the congregation in chairs sloped up to the back wall. Behind him was a white board covered with biblical quotations, notes, and hastily sketched illustrations in a variety of colors. His face was hidden behind the large sunglasses that he wore almost constantly in those days. He was dressed in a comfortable old sweater, ragged around the neckline, with numerous holes and stains, and an old pair of blue jeans and cowboy boots.

"I've told you that I've been close to death all my life. Death has been my constant companion all through this mortal life. I was close to death when I was born and I've lived with death all my life. But I am not afraid of death. I've been in car accidents that should have killed me. I've been shot.

I've been stabbed. I've been beaten. The whole of my life, this life that I'm living now, has been a trial run for my death. But I'm not afraid of death, I tell you. I'm not afraid of death because I've been dead and I have lived. Again and again. I have been dead and lived again. I know death just about as well as I know life. And what I know is this: Until you embrace the meaning of death, you won't have a clue about the meaning of life."

He ran his hands through his short hair and smiled. The member of the community leaned in closer, ready to hear his words. Ready to receive his message.

"Once, when I was a boy, a young teenager, I went swimming in a local river with some friends. We often went there to fish and swim during the summer. One of my friend's older brother had rigged up a rope swing for us—a thick rope tied to a tree branch that hung out over the water. We would swing out on that rope and at the apex of the arc, we'd let go and go splashing into the water. It was great fun. But on this particular occasion when I went into the water, I hit something under the surface—a rock, or a log, or submerged shopping car, I don't know what it might have been - but I was knocked out. Completely unconscious. And my unconscious body began floating down the current of the river."

The congregation leaned in closer now, captivated by his story. The air in the auditorium was stuffy and warm, but the individuals gathered there didn't seem to notice. They were caught up and enthralled by their leader's experience.

"The boys that I was with dove into the water to rescue me. I wasn't swimming. I wasn't breathing. I was just floating downstream. They swam out to me and dragged me back to the shore. One of them ran to a nearby house to call for an ambulance. I don't really remember any of this, of course. They told me about it afterwards. I don't remember any of this because by that time I was already leaving my body."

"And as I was leaving my body, I began to see a vision. In that moment, even as my physical body was dying for a lack of oxygen, I was seeing the celestial sights. I saw the bright lights that you hear about in so many incidents of this kind. I saw the glory of heaven all around me. I saw the eternal circle of light from one end of the horizon to the other and back around again. But, what was more important, what was more impressive to me in that moment was what I was hearing. I heard a humming sound that I could not, and still cannot explain. It was a humming that seemed to come from every point of the universe at once. And it seemed that there were words in that humming. I couldn't understand what the words were saying, but I could recognize them as speech of some sort. I can still remember the syllables that formed those words. I can hear them in my head."

The audience murmured, amazed. They wanted to hear these words. They were ready to hear and to receive, ready to be shaped by them.

"I can still remember the exact sound of those words, every single syllable, " DK told them. "But I will not repeat them. Not in this life—for I believe them to be holy words. Profound and sacred words that should not be spoken by mere human lips. I dare not repeat them in this life. Like the prophet Isaiah said, 'Woe is me for I am a man of unclean lips.'"

The audience sighed, disappointed, but sill no less intrigued. They remained caught up in the report of the vision. They longed to share the vision with their leader, to join with him in the recollection of this mystical experience.

"And the sound of the humming began to crescendo. It was getting louder and louder all around me, to the point that I began to worry that my ear drums would burst. But I wasn't thinking clearly, of course. My ears were still with my body in the back of the ambulance as it raced toward the hospital. But that humming sound was so loud I thought that I was going to explode. Then suddenly, abruptly the humming sound was cut off. Silenced. I was enveloped in complete silence. And the golden light began to dim until all was dark. All was darkness and silence. It was a void stretching out in all directions. And, even more, the silence and the darkness seemed to fill me completely. There was nothing but silence and darkness. I was nothing but silence and darkness."

"Now most of the verses in the Bible that use the word 'silence' are from people imploring God to not be silent. They were calling on him to speak and to not be silent. they were calling on him to come to their aid and their rescue. Silence—in most of the Bible, as we have it today—is seen as the absence of God's holy presence. But I began to wonder—how can the omnipresent, transcendent God truly be absent? Even in the silence. It was then that I came to understand that silence is not the absence of God, but instead is the full, unmediated expression of the divine voice, just as the prophet Elijah came to understand that God was not in the wind, or the earthquake, or the burning fire. God came to Elijah in the 'still, small voice.' It was the silent voice of God."

"It was the silence that spoke to me—the sound of silence, the silent voice. And in that moment, in that moment of overwhelming darkness and silence, I knew exactly who I was. I knew who I'd been. But I didn't understand yet what I was called to do in this life. That understanding came later, after I'd died again."

The members of the congregation sighed and looked at each other in wonder and amazement. But none of them could say anything.

* * *

"Given DK's pattern of manipulation and deception, do you believe that he actually experienced these near death experiences that he claimed to have had?" Myron asks me.

"Why would he lie?"

"It's what he did, Travis. He told people stories to manipulate them, to motivate them to give him money, or to do favors for him. It's what he did, repeatedly throughout his life."

"Why would he lie?" I ask again. I am annoyed with Myron. "I never knew him to lie to me, or to anyone." I say this but something, somewhere in the back of my mind wonders.

"We have his childhood records and there's nothing to indicate that he was rescued from a river or that he nearly died of asphyxiation. There's no hospital record, no record of transport in an ambulance. There's nothing in the local paper of that time about it. There's nothing at all about this incident."

"I don't know."

"Come on, Travis . . . "

"I don't know. And I don't want to say any more."

"Okay. Okay," Myron says. "Let's take a break for a few minutes. We'll get you a glass of water."

Chapter Seven

THE HEAT OF THE day lingered well into the night, but there was a breeze. Crickets chirped somewhere in the desert brush at the edge of the compound. The shadow of the Superstition Mountains stretched out across the sand and rock and cactus of the desert. Travis had finished his chores and was drinking a soda as he walked across the lot to the trailer where he shared a room with four other members of the community. But a noise caught his attention. Even though it was softer than the cricket's chirrup, he could hear someone crying. A woman. He could hear a woman crying.

Under the light of a small lamp by the kitchen door he saw Maggie sobbing with her hands covering her face. Her body heaved and quivered with each burst of tears. He wondered if he should approach. He wondered if he should flee. He wondered if he should speak or be silent.

"Ms. Snow," Travis said finally with a squeaky and hesitating voice. "Ms. Snow, I'm sorry. I didn't mean to . . . " He stopped. He'd run out of words. He didn't know what to do or say. "I'm sorry."

"Travis," she said. "No. It's okay."

"Are you sure?" he asked.

She laughed and sniffed, a wet snotty sound. She wiped her face with her hands. "Ah well. . . Okay is relative, I guess." She gave him a broken smile and said, "I'm okay. I'm just sad. And the sadness will pass. It always does."

Travis sat down next to her. "Why are you so sad?"

Maggie wiped her eyes again and brushed her hair away from her face where it had been plastered by her tears to her cheeks. "Part of me still misses my ex-husband, Gracie's father. It's been a couple of years since he left us, but I still miss him."

"I get that. I still miss my mom. But I thought you said he hurt you."

"Yeah," she said. "He was hurtful to me and to our little girl, and I wouldn't put myself or Gracie back into that relationship—but I loved him once. Still do, I suppose. Though I don't know why. He left a hole in my heart when he abandoned us."

Neither of them said anything for a few minutes, then Maggie continued. "Part of me died when he left, I think. Part of me died. And every now and again, I still grieve that death." They sat together in the dark listening to the crickets and the breeze in the brush. Travis reached over and held her hand as she cried. And they sat together for a long time, long after the moon rose into the dark sky.

* * *

[From a transcript of a cassette tape recording of Bible study session—August 1992]

[Reverend DK strums an electric guitar]

[Reverend DK] I want to play a song for you. A song I wrote. The idea for this song came to me one morning, about ten years ago—a little more than ten years ago, when I was walking around the lake in an early morning, autumn fog in a small town in southern Minnesota. The orange and red leaves of the trees burned in the silver fog. The melody of the Methodist church bells and the backup alarm of a city garbage truck merged in the mist. I couldn't see either the church or the garbage truck. I couldn't locate them in physical space—everything was lost in that fog. But I could hear them. The melodious bells and the harsh mechanical alarm of the truck seemed to be one sonorous object. And that's when the words came to me.

Not that the words have anything to do with that particular experience. It's just a very vivid memory for me—the colors of the leaves against the fog, the cool damp air. I remember the whole scene. I was alive—wholly alive - in that moment.

I didn't write the music for it until a few years later, when I was down in Nashville. At that time I thought I'd take a stab at being a rock star. I was playing with a band called Loose Change and Whiskey in the clubs during the nights and working as a studio musician during the day. I recorded a demo with a few buddies, but even though five different record executives came out to talk to me about a recording contract, none of them actually delivered on their grandiose promises.

This song wasn't on the demo that we recorded, but here's *Emerge from this Alive.*

[DK strums the guitar again and sings]

Everything's ready
but the hours drag on
and then there's nothing
the doctor's gone home.
Don't wait for morning
if she's still alive.
Tomorrow's too late,
there's a crisis tonight.
We will never
emerge from this alive.
We will never
emerge from this alive.
All of the angels
in this room
sounding their trumpets
to send us on.
What's happened here
must not be heard
so guard this secret
with your lives.
We will never
emerge from this alive.
We will never
emerge from this alive.
The mood is grim
we're spitting up blood
that's what can happen
in times like these.
A time is coming
for cosmic fire
so let the light
of your soul shine.
We will never
emerge from this alive.

We will never
emerge from this alive.

[Applause from the congregation]
[End transcript]

* * *

"The people of Zion's Freedom like DK's music. He played really well.

"Yeah. He was an excellent musician, but not much of a songwriter," Myron says.

"What do you mean? He wrote a bunch of hymns and songs that he played for our worship times. We liked singing them."

"Well he might not have actually written most of them," Myron tells me. "That last one was actually written by one of DK's band-mates. Loose Change and Whiskey recorded it for their debut album after DK left Nashville.

"Oh yeah?" This isn't something I'd heard before. After all these years, Myron is challenging what I thought I knew of DK. "Did he write any of them at all?"

"Well," Myron hesitates. "It's difficult to say for sure. There is one song that we can't find any other source for. He may have written it. Do you remember a song he played called *The World So Dark?*"

I don't remember it. But it's been a long, long time. I shake my head no.

"Dave," Myron calls to his assistant. "Do you have that song file on your laptop?" Dave says that he does. They play it for me. And I do remember hearing DK play it for us. I liked it then. I still do. It's a good song.

* * *

[DK song file *The World So Dark*—DK singing and playing the guitar]

Darkness speaks of foolish things
interest lost in pawnshop rings.
Close the door on the world so dark.

Drop the number, lose the name
changing now from flesh to flame.
Leave behind the world so dark.

Power in a still beating heart
lightning so bright shadows depart.

Take the wind and take the rain
take away the wasted pain.
Close the door on the world so dark.

Trade the laughter for the tears
all the things we hold dear
Leave behind the world so dark.

What is broken can be repaired
most of what we fear was never there.

Darkness speak of foolish things
interest lost in pawnshop rings.
Close the door on the world so dark.

Drop the number, lose the name
changing now from flesh to flame.
Leave behind the world so dark.

* * *

"Thanks," I say to Myron. "It's good to hear that song again."

Myron continues the interview. "From what you've told me, and what you've said in our previous discussions, and in the few interviews you've given to other reporters, it seems that in the short time that you were at Zion's Freedom, you and Reverend DK developed a special relationship. He was fatherly toward you," Myron says. "Tell me something about that. I know he taught you about motorcycles. What else? Did he impart any wisdom to you? Life lessons?"

"He taught me a couple of magic tricks. Wanna' see?"

"Sure. That would be awesome, Travis."

I ask if he has a coin, but he doesn't have one. The cameraman says that he has an extra battery for his light meter and that it is flat and round and about the size of a coin. It will work. After he hands me the coin shaped battery I hold it up for them to see, between the thumb and pointer finger of my right hand. "It's an ordinary coin, right?" I say and they chuckle. And then I put the coin into my left hand and wave both hands back and forth. But when I open my left hand the battery is not there. It's still in my right hand.

"That's pretty good, Travis," Myron says. "My nephew wants to be a magician so he shows me all the tricks he learns. He's shown me this one. I think every amateur prestidigitator learns it. But it really looked like you had the battery in your left hand. You had me fooled."

"DK told me that it's not just about doing the right things with your hands—hiding the coin your hands is the easy part. DK told me that the hard part, the necessary part of the trick, is all the other stuff. The way you stand, your posture, your breathing, the tone of your voice, where you're looking, everything. You have to set the whole scene, not just what you're doing or not doing with your hands. The whole thing has to appear natural."

"That's very interesting," Myron says. "Can you perform any other illusions?"

"I know a couple of card tricks. Do you have a deck of cards?" Neither Myron or his cameraman have any playing cards with them so I can't show them the other tricks I know. But that's okay. The coin trick is my best one anyway.

* * *

DK and Travis rode into town on DK's motorcycle for dinner—burgers, fries and a coke at McDonald's. They sat in the air conditioned restaurant to share their meal. "How are you enjoying Zion's Freedom?" DK asked after eating a bite of his burger.

"It's great," Travis said. "Everyone's really nice." Travis shoved another handful of fries into his mouth.

"I'm glad to hear that," DK said. "Because everyone there really likes you as well. You've quickly become a treasured part of our family. We're all very glad you've been with us the past couple of months. But I want you to know that, as much as we all like you and want you to stay with us, you are free to leave whenever you want. It will be your choice, Travis. Your decision."

"I don't want to go," Travis said. "Besides," he added after a mouthful of cola, "where could I go? I've got no other family, besides Aunt Carol in Chicago, but I hardly know her. And I don't want to be put in a foster home. I don't want to go anywhere else. I like it here."

"That's good," DK said. "That's great. Because I truly believe that God led you to us. It wasn't just a random coincidence. It wasn't blind fate. It was the mighty moving hand of God. The world out there is crazy and getting crazier every day. But here you are. With us. And for that we are blessed. I thank God for you, Triple-T."

Travis grinned and took another huge bite of his burger.

Later, after they'd finished their food and were lingering over refilled beverages, DK asked Travis another question. "Tell me, Triple-T, do you have a girlfriend? Anyone in particular that you're interested in?" Travis blushed. "I thought so," DK said.

"I don't have a girlfriend," Travis said a little too loudly, too quickly and spilled some of his soda.

"I get it," DK said. "I get it. It's okay. That first love is awkward and exhilarating. Your hands tremble and sweat. Your heart pounds. Your stomach feels like it's going to turn inside out. And your throat clenches up when she's not around, yeah? Is that how it is for you, son?"

"Yeah," Travis acknowledged and blushed again. "Yeah. I mean, she's just so pretty. I don't know what to say when I'm around her."

"I remember how it felt being in love."

"What was it like?" Travis asked. "How did you know you were in love?"

DK took another sip of his soda and looked off into the distance. "It was while I was in college, in Minnesota. This girl—her name was Michelle—and I had been friends for a while, but I started to feel. . . different about her. I didn't understand that change at first, I just knew I enjoyed spending time with her. And I wanted to be with her all the time. We were walking together across the quad one time—it was winter—and we were feeling goofy so we started into a snowball fight by the campus bell tower."

"And that's when you knew?"

"It was the way she laughed when she pelted me with one of those snowballs. She got me right in the face. She laughed and that's when I knew that I loved her. And I thought she loved me . . . "

"What happened?"

"I don't really know. We were together for a couple of years, but she just sorta' shut down on me. She stopped talking to me. She stopped wanting to be around me. I don't know why." He paused and sighed. "But it doesn't really matter now. This life that I'm living isn't one where I have the luxury or freedom to love as I might please. You understand? Like the apostle Paul, I'm too busy to be married. If I were married I would have to spend all my time trying to please my wife. Those who are married will have trouble in this life and I just can't have that. I need to be free of all distractions so that I can focus all my energies on my work. There are so many things I have to accomplish while I'm here and there never seems to be enough time to do them all. We don't have much time left now."

DK sighed and looked at Travis again. "But I do remember what it was like to be young and in love," he went on. "I remember the thrill and excitement of a young romance."

"What should I do?" Travis asked. "Should I tell her how I feel?"

"Don't worry," DK said. "When the time is right you'll know exactly what you should do."

"But what if she . . . "

"Nevermind all the maybes and what-ifs. They're nothing but the distractions of anxiety. Fear and anxiety are diseases. Fear and anxiety are infections of the soul. Do not be anxious about girls, Triple-T. For now, just wait. Just listen for the voice of silence and when the time is right you'll find the words you need to tell her how you feel."

"I don't know, DK . . . "

"But I do. I know. I know."

* * *

"The second time I died," DK said to his audience, "the second time I died in this life, I was working in Ohio."

It was another evening Bible study in the compound, another marathon session of biblical lecture. DK had begun that evening with a text from the prophet Isaiah, but had quickly veered away from the words of the prophet into a long and rambling digression on the words, "Forget the former things; do not dwell on the past. See, I am doing a new thing." Later some of the members of his congregation would attempt to retrace the course of the lecture by comparing their notes. But they couldn't remember all the various connections and associations he'd made over the course of those hours. But it was no matter to them. They accepted it as a weakness of their memories and pledged to pay closer attention in the next session

"I was twenty-three and working in a lumber yard—which may not have been the most glamorous of professions but it certainly paid the bills. And hey, Jesus was a carpenter, right? So maybe it was appropriate. Anyway, I was working in a lumber yard, and very quickly, over the course of just a couple of weeks, I began developing a number of bizarre medical symptoms."

"I had severe abdominal pains—massive cramps that would leave me crying and writhing on the floor, screaming in pain. And I developed these weird lumps on my neck. My doctor couldn't figure out what they were, but they were inflamed and painful to the touch. Like giant spider bites. And on top of that, I was tired all the time. Just exhausted. There were days when I couldn't even find the energy to get out of bed to go to the bathroom. I just lay there and pissed myself because I didn't have the energy to get up. Eventually my roommate took me to the emergency room because I was struggling to breath. That's when they discovered that my entire body was completely shutting down. My liver, my kidneys, my lungs. Even the marrow in my bones was shutting down. Everything. All at once."

"Later, after I came back, they said it was some sort of unknown autoimmune disease. That was as close as they could get to a diagnosis. An unknown autoimmune disease. They said that my immune system, for no explicable reason, began to attack my own body. And they couldn't explain it. They didn't understand it, even with all their medical degrees. Neither could they explain why all the symptoms disappeared as suddenly as they'd begun. It was all a huge medical mystery."

"What you need to understand is that death is a process. It's more like a line than a single point in time. And at either end of this line there are two poles. One pole is your normal, waking reality, your everyday life. At the other end of the line is irreversible death from which there is no return. Usually, but not always. There are some exceptions. Brain death is closer to this pole, but not the same as irreversible death. A lack of brain wave activity is not necessarily the same thing as physical death. Brain dead isn't completely dead." He paused and gave the congregation a sly look and added, "You just look at some of our politicians if you want to understand that." His followers chuckled.

"What happened to me, and to countless others who've had a near death experience, is not merely a physical, chemical experience. It's not just some random, spasmodic electrical discharge in the brain. It's not just a seizure. It wasn't the result of a lack of oxygen to my brain. This was real. This death was real life—so to speak."

"But while I was in the hospital, with every organ in my body shutting down, I lapsed into a coma for a couple of days. It was during those days that I saw the celestial sights again. And I heard that voice of silence again. It said to me, 'You are my witness and my servant. You are the silence that I have chosen I say this to you so that you will know, and believe, and understand. Before me there is no other. After you there will be no other.' That's what the silence said to me."

"But there was more that came to me in that silence—though it didn't come all at once. The message that I began to receive during those days when my body was in a comatose state has been growing in me ever since. I didn't understand it all at once. It took time. But now we are close. Now we are near to a full understanding. And it is this: Zion is a secret—the secret life after life reserved for the righteous and the pure. It is a place prepared for the elect of God It is Enoch's City - Enoch lived three hundred and sixty-five years before he was taken by God. He was taken somewhere."

"And this isn't just figurative. He wasn't just taken to some spiritual place. He was taken to a real place. A physical place here on earth. And it took me a long time to realize what this means and it took me even longer to find the place where he was taken. But now we have found it. It's not far from here. That's why we chose this location. That's why we have built the Zion's Freedom compound here. The silent voice of the Lord whispered the location to me, just as he whispered to me the names of those who are ready to go to Zion."

Chapter Eight

"TELL ME ABOUT THE show *Studies in Silence,*" Myron says. I can't see him through the glare of the lights but he sounds like he's grinning. And I know what he's talking about. I remember that one. It was fun.

"That was the show that DK pitched to Channel Forty-Nine down in Tucson," I tell him. "DK thought he could start a Bible study program to watch on TV. He rented a camera and some other equipment. I helped set up the lights and microphones for him."

"Why did DK want to get into television programming? Was he trying to be like one of the televangelists like Pat Robertson or Jim Bakker? Or Jack Van Impe, maybe?"

"No. He never said anything good about those guys on TV. No. He just wanted a way to tell people the truth about the Bible. And he was pretty mad too, about that Satan program that Channel Forty-Nine broadcast earlier that year."

"That would be the program *The Great Satan at Large* by Lou Perfidio, right?"

"I don't remember the guy's name, but *Great Satan at Large,* that sounds right."

"Yeah, that was Lou Perfidio. He died several years ago of some infection, I think. That show is legendary in some circles," Myron says. "Did you see it yourself?"

"No. We only had one TV at the compound and that was mostly for the kids to watch movies. The adults used it sometimes, but not often. We didn't have a phone or the internet either. DK said that we didn't need their distractions or their interference. And DK said that if the heathens down in Tucson were willing to show a program about the devil, with pictures of Hitler and strippers and masturbating jesters, then they sure as shootin' should have been willing to put up a program of Bible studies."

"I thought you said that you didn't see *The Great Satan at Large* broadcast . . . "

"I didn't. Like I said, we really didn't watch much television. DK told us all that we needed to know about it."

"So he saw it?"

"I guess he must have. Anyways, we filmed . . . what do you call it?"

"A pilot episode?" Myron suggests, and he's right.

"Yeah, a pilot episode. But the station turned him down. They didn't want to broadcast it. They said that they couldn't air religious programming. DK tried reminding them that they'd just put up the *Great Satan* show and that Satanism was a religion too. But they still said no. And they didn't even send him the tape back."

"I've tried to locate a copy of DK's *Studies in Silence* program," Myron tells me, "but I haven't been able to find one. I don't know what they did with it, but Channel Forty-Nine didn't retain a copy of it. And if there was another copy at the compound, it was destroyed in the fire. What was the format of DK's program?"

"What do you mean?"

"What kind of program was it?"

"Oh," I understand what he means now. "Basically it was the same kind of material he used in his evening lectures to the group but he didn't go on quite as long. I helped set up the lights and microphones in the little studio he fixed up at the compound."

"You said that. How did he take the rejection from Channel Forty-Nine?"

"Well, he wasn't happy about it."

"No. I should guess he wasn't."

"He said it was his own damned fault and that he should have known that the Prince of the Power of the Air was still the spirit that worked in the children of disobedience who controlled the media."

* * *

[From a transcript of a cassette tape recording of Reverend DK sermon—September 1992]

[Reverend DK] All of our delusions and all of our confusions in this life arise from the limitations and the failures of our physical beings. Our senses are limited. We do not see clearly. We do not hear distinctly. We barely smell anything unless it is overwhelmingly pungent or cloyingly sweet. The animals hear, and see, and smell the world better than we do. All that we experience in this life is distorted by the limitations of our physical senses. And what we remember of those experiences is further distorted by the vagaries of our memory. We do not remember objectively or correctly. So why should we be surprised that we don't understand the world?

So I ask you again: What is life like—and why live it at all?

[Long moment of silence]

[Reverend DK] I mean it. What answer will you give me? What is life like and why should we bother to live it at all?

[Another long silence]

[Reverend DK] Does none of you have an answer for me for this question? Anyone? Does any one of you understand how vitally important this is? This is the most important question there is. One could say that this is the only question. What is life and why should we live it at all?

Come on. . . Anyone? What about you Christoph? You and I talked about this for an hour just this morning while your wife and kids were at the zoo.

[Christoph James] I. . . I. . . I. . .

[Reverend DK] I. . . I. . . I. . . what? Did you forget already? Does the time I gave you, the time I spend answering your questions mean so little to you that you can't be bothered to pay attention to what I'm trying to tell you?

Does anyone have a goddamned clue what I'm talking about up here? No? None of you? All right then, perhaps we should just call it quits. Maybe we should just give up. At least for tonight. The crown is always worn on a trembling head. It is the weight of burden and the fear of the guillotine. The world has assassinated me over and over again. And I don't think that any of you really care. Go to bed, everyone. I'm tied. I'm done with you. Go to bed. We'll try again in the morning.

[End transcript]

* * *

The next morning's breakfast—pancakes and oatmeal, again prepared by Maggie Snow and Opal Mills—was subdued and mostly silent. Marsha and Gary Matthews held a whispered conversation with their two children—Luke, who was eight years old and Emily, who was five. The children were reluctant to eat the yogurt and fruit that had been given to them. Marsha and Gary were urgently, but quietly, trying to coax them into eating without disturbing the silence. The rest of the community stared sullenly at their bowls of oatmeal or their cups of coffee.

Travis ate his breakfast quickly and went back to the serving counter for seconds. Maggie served him another large helping of the homemade yogurt and berries grown in the community's gardens. Travis thanked her quietly and smiled at her. "You're welcome, Travis. Go sit quietly with your meal. DK will be down to speak to us soon," she told him.

But he wasn't.

The members of the congregation waited for their leader to speak to them, but there were chores to be done and jobs to get to. Those with jobs outside the compound excused themselves and left the grounds. Eventually the tables were cleared, the dishes were washed. The children were shuffled off with Miss Louisa to the home school room. Mark Kemper went to his job at Thompson Brothers' Contracting—they were renovating an apartment building that month. His wife, Claudia, went to her position as part of the horticulture staff at the Boyce Thompson Arboretum. Emmett Fischer went to his job at the Superior Town Sewage plant. Most mornings he would finish his coffee and joke, "It's a shitty job, but someone has to do it." But not this day. There were no jokes that morning and only a few whispered goodbyes as each of them departed to their various responsibilities.

Travis volunteered to help clear tables and wash dishes. He didn't have a regularly assigned duty with the compound or a job on the outside like the adults. He wasn't going to school in Superior and he was certainly too old to be shuffled off with the little ones in Miss Louisa's care, but he liked to be helpful. He wanted to do his part to be part of the group so he frequently offered to help with kitchen duties.

"Where's DK this morning?" he asked Maggie as he stood next to her, drying the last of the dishes. Opal had already gone off to work in the gardens before it got too hot to pull weeds.

"I don't know, Travis," Maggie told him as she took the plates and put them into the cupboard. "No one's seen him this morning, but none of the compound's vehicles are missing. And that old motorcycle of his is still here. He's probably hiked up the mountain. He does that sometimes. Sometimes he just needs to get away. Sometimes he just needs to go out into the wilderness like Jesus did."

"Should we . . . " he began. "Do you think he needs . . . " he tried again.

"No. No," she assured him. "Sometimes he just needs to be alone to find his silence. He'll be back soon enough. Probably before lunch."

But he wasn't. The lunch hour rolled around and DK still had not returned. So Travis decided that he would go out looking for him. He laced his tennis shoes up tight and put on a ball cap to keep the sun out of his eyes. He filled his backpack with granola bars and bottled water and hiked out of the compound on the trail that led up into the mountains. He went east first, toward Queen Creek and then turned north passing under US Route Sixty on the Queen Creek Viaduct. He thought he might go as far as the abandoned Magma copper mine shafts, but he encountered DK coming in the opposite direction.

"Hail and well met, fellow traveler," DK called out to him. Travis saw him a long way off and ran to him. The two of them met in a tremendous embrace.

"I was worried when you didn't come back. I brought water," Travis said in a rush as he set his pack down and started unzipping it to bring out the water he'd carried with him. "They won't be cold anymore, but they're still wet." He handed two of the bottles to DK.

"Triple-T, you are a godsend," DK said as he cracked open one of the bottles and drank the entire thing in a long succession of chugs. "You are a godsend and a blessing, son."

"Where were you?"

"DK patted Travis on the shoulder and smiled. "I went up to a sacred place I know. It's secluded and quiet, pretty well hidden It's a secret spot and no one else knows about it. That's where I go when I need to hear from the divine. So I laid myself upon the ground and purified my heart by quieting my senses and subduing my mind by fixing it on one, single point."

The two of them found a shady spot and sat down to share more of the water and to eat a couple of the granola bars Travis had brought with him. As they shared this impromptu communion, DK spoke to Travis. "The glory of the shining sun—the light and heat that dispels the chill of gloomy dark—this light comes from God. And the glory of the silver moon in the dark, this too is from God. The light is one light. It all comes from God, you see?"

"Uh . . . sure," Travis said. "I get it. One light."

"Do you?" DK asked with a piercing eye on Travis. "Do you really?" He sighed. "No. I think you want to understand, but you don't. Not yet. Don't worry, though," he said as his gaze softened. "It doesn't matter. Not really. Everything's happening too fast. It's all happening too fast, Triple-T. It's all coming too fast."

"You're right, DK," Travis said. "I don't understand. Not really. But I'm trying to understand, DK. I'm trying as hard as I can to understand what you say."

DK tousled his hair and took another large chug of water. "Don't worry about it at all, son. You shouldn't have to worry about anything Triple-T. You should never have to worry about anything."

* * *

"This would have been about the time that you had a couple of investigators come to ask questions at the Zion's Freedom compound. The first was an agent from Child Protective Services, right? Her name was Justine Bacon?"

"Heh. Heh. Yeah. I remember her name. She had it on a name tag when she came out to the compound. She told DK that I needed to be enrolled in school and that I was already considered truant. She said it was unlawful for me to miss school. That was the word she used—unlawful. She also said something about how it was unclear if DK and Zion's Freedom was providing enough for my welfare and education. She also said it wasn't clear if he had any right to my custody and that I would need to be placed into a proper foster home until the question could be resolved."

"What did DK do?"

"He told her off. He said, 'Just because you folks in the child welfare department have finally remembered him after all this time doesn't give you any justification to come out here to our home.' He told her that God had seen fit to bring me to Zion's Freedom and that they were all the family I needed. Then he noticed her name tag and said, 'I suggest, Ms. Bacon, that you take your piggy self and turn right around on your ham hocks and get out of here.' I laughed pretty hard at that then, but it seems kinda' cruel now when I think about it."

"Yeah. He had an acerbic tongue sometimes, didn't he?" Myron says.

"I don't know that word."

"It means sharply critical. He could be a bit mean spirited."

"Yeah, sometimes," I agree.

"And it was only a few days after this incident that the FBI agents, Marcus and Ramirez, returned to ask DK more questions about the murdered Marla Glenn. Is that correct?"

"Yeah. That really freaked DK out. It got weird in the camp after that."

* * *

[From a transcript of a cassette tape recording of Reverend DK sermon—September 1992]

[Reverend DK] This is what I've been saying. This is what I've told you would happen. Do you see? Do you understand? They've come to take away our Triple-T. They've come to take away the young man that the Lord God himself put into our care. How long will it be before they send out more of their godless child protective service agents to take away our other babies? Do you want them to come for your precious little boy, Stephanie?

[Stephanie Lewis] I won't let them take my little Chad, DK. You know that's God's own truth!

[Reverend DK] I know it's true, Stephanie. I know it. And how about you, Marsha and Gary? Are you willing to let them come in here and take Luke and Emily from you?

[Gary Matthews] No!

[Marsha Matthews] Absolutely Not!

[Reverend DK] It's happening now. Or it soon will be. It's all happening so fast, and it's all happening at once. I can't control it. I can't slow it down. They're coming for our children, and soon they'll be coming for you. They'll be coming for me too. They'll be coming to take your children from you, but they'll be coming to kill me. We need to be ready to go up the mountain to the fortress that is being prepared for us. To a cleft in the rock that is higher. . .

[Long applause]

[Reverend DK] But I'm so tired, people. I'm so tired. It's like I'm trying to pull a two ton stone up from the bottom of a deep well. I can't do it. I just can't do it. And I'm a strong guy, right? I exercise. I work out. I lift weights with some of you men. You know how strong I am, yeah? You've all seen me in the exercise room. But I can't do this. It's just too much. It's too heavy for one man.

I want to be done, but I've got too much that I still need to do. I need all the minutes and the hours that are left to me. I need every day that I have left.

[End transcript]

* * *

Not far from Superior, Arizona, in the town of Apache Junction, there is a place where—twice a year, in the spring and the autumn—the sun will strike the Superstition Mountains in such a way as to cast the shadow of a cougar across the face of the mountain. The cougar only appears twice a year for about a week, just as the sun is setting. This phenomenon only occurs when the sun sets at just the right latitude on the western horizon. The last thirty minutes before official sunset is prime time for viewing the shadow cougar, and people from all over the world line the sides of the road to watch with binoculars and cameras as the cougar creeps across the side of the mountain in the orange glow of sunset. DK and Travis rode out to Apache Junction on the motorcycle that had carried them across the south-western deserts and up and down mountain roads. They went to see the shadow of the cougar.

They parked the motorcycle on the shoulder of the road, along with a line of other cars and minivans and motorcycles. Families had come with their children. Men and women came holding hands to see watch as the light from the sun, ninety-three million miles away, in the western sky created the shadow of the mountain lion the face of the mountain.

"Visionaries can often see what other cannot," DK told Travis as they watched the great cat stretch languidly across the rock face. "You and I are not living like these others here. The world is going to hell, but we can see the way out. We know what is necessary."

"What is it," Travis asked. "What is the necessary thing?"

DK smiled and said, "Right now, sleep is the necessary thing. 'Sleep, the thing before whom all things bow,' as Homer once said.

"Homer Simpson?"

He laughed at the boy's misapprehension. "No, son. Not that Homer." DK pointed to the shadow on the mountain and said, "Behold, and do not weep, the lion, the mountain lion, of Judah. He is able to open the scroll and its seven seals."

"What does it mean?" Travis asked, his voice hushed and reverent.

"Nothing much. I was mostly making a joke. Though among some of the indigenous people of this area, the wail of the mountain lion is believed to be the harbinger of death. I've seen their petroglyphs carved into the stones out in the desert. I've read their apocalyptic warnings of death and destruction. I've known death my whole life, so this is not new to me. But I'm tired, son. I'm so tired."

They watched until the sun had set and the shadow of the cougar had blended into the growing gloaming and all was dark of night. "Let's go home, Triple-T. I need to sleep."

Chapter Nine

THE NOSEBLEED WAS NOT severe and Travis had the bleeding under control quickly. There was little blood spilled, but he cleaned it from the floor and comforted little Gracie until her mother returned home. He gave her a bowl of ice cream and the two of them watched movies on the daycare television until Maggie got home. Little kids get nosebleeds all the time and Travis understood this. He wasn't overly excited by the accident and he didn't scare Gracie. She responded to his calm with a calm of her own.

Ms. Snow had to go to Flagstaff to visit her lawyer to go over some court documents concerning her custody of Gracie, so she'd asked if Travis would watch her while she was gone. She promised that she'd be back that evening. Travis agreed readily. He'd have done anything for Ms. Snow and besides, he liked Gracie. Everyone did. She was a pretty child, perpetually happy and always laughing. She laughed at the insects that buzzed around her and smiled at the flowers growing at her feet. She waved to the clouds in the sky and sang songs for the sun. How could anyone not love a precocious child like that?

And she loved to run. She ran everywhere. "I'm fast," she'd scream as she ran with her arms stretched out from her sides like airplane wings. "Fast as the wiiiiinnnnnnnd!" That afternoon she was running in great circles around the play yard yelling out, "I'm faaaaaaasssssssst!" But like little kids everywhere she was often unsteady on her feet.

"Careful, Gracie," Travis cautioned. She tripped over a stuffed animal left lying on the ground even before Travis had finished urging her to caution. She stumbled and smacked her face against one of the plastic playground slides that the Zion's Freedom compound kept for the children to play on, and gave herself a bloody nose. She didn't cry right away. Not until she saw the blood. Then she wailed and tears flooded from her eyes.

Travis rushed to pick her up and to quiet her crying. "It's okay," he told her. "It's okay, Gracie. It's only blood." And that made her giggle. He told her to pinch her nostrils closed and he carried her inside to the bathroom where he washed her face. A few drops of blood dribbled on the floor, but he cleaned that up too.

"It's only blood," Gracie told him and they both laughed.

That's when Travis saw DK standing in the hall outside the bathroom. He'd been watching as Travis wiped the tears from the girl's face and cleaned up the blood. "She tripped and banged her face," Travis explained. "But I think she'll be okay."

"I saw what happened," DK said.

"It's only blood," Gracie said and laughed again.

"Travis," DK called and then motioned for him. "Come here for a moment."

"Keep that pinched tight, Sweetie. I'll be right back," Travis whispered to Gracie and then excused himself to see what DK wanted.

"You're going to have to keep a careful eye on her," DK said sternly. "Independent girls are the worry of the church. Independent boys can be broken and pulled into line. They're like horses that way. But independent girls are always trouble. Keep an eye on her." He looked Travis in the eyes and put his hands on Travis' shoulders. "Do you hear what I'm saying to you?"

Travis nodded and took Gracie to the kitchen to get her a bowl of chocolate ice cream.

* * *

"DK became increasingly erratic at the end. Listening to recordings of his sermons and Bible studies is like listening to some sort of surreal, apocalyptic poetry. They're filled with non-sequiturs and discontinuities." Myron uses big words that I don't understand. He tries to explain to me about rhetorical devices and something called anacoluthon—which sounds like it should be a snake, but he says it isn't. I don't know what he means by erratic.

"I didn't understand all the stuff that he taught, but he was a smart man. I know that. He knew all kinds of things that no one else knew."

"You didn't think that he might have been slipping a little towards the end? Was he getting a little weird?"

"He was tired, that's all." He had a lot of pressure on him. We were all tired."

* * *

[From a transcript of a cassette tape recording of Reverend DK sermon—October 1992]

[Reverend DK] Why do you lie? Why do you lie since you belong to me? Tell the truth. The truth will set you free. I saw you. I see you. I know you. I knew you—though you did not and do not see or recognize yourselves. I was as close to you as the shirt you wear, but you never even felt me.

Listen to me. Do you hear me? You are nothing but second rate devils—thrift store Satans. And from here on out it can only be rebellion and the eternally advancing wrath of God for you and yours. You are moving inevitably toward vindictive jealousy and the wrath of God. Can't you understand this? Cant you see what is happening?   It's fever for one hour and fear forever.

The glory of the shining sun—the light that dispels the gloomy dark— this light comes from God. And the glory of the silver moon in the dark, this too comes from God. The light is one light But you are blind and you see neither. You see nothing and you understand even less.

I could be anyone, anybody. Dangerous. I could be dangerous. You don't know. I could be deadly. There's a fine line between paranoia and awareness. We're all evil somewhere inside. And there is no choice. Death comes for everyone. Death is the territory we all pass through. But when? That's the real question. That's the sixty-four thousand dollar question. We start dying the moment we're born. As one of the poets said somewhere, "We are wounded in birth and bleed to death."

Something has gone sour. Something has rotted. Something has died beneath the porch and the stench of its putrification is overwhelming Something has died—but it's not me. I've died and been reborn hundreds of times, but it's not me. Not this time. All things perish and wither and fade. But I am still alive, at least for now.

Listen to this. Listen to me. Satanic speculation develops intentionally and internationally—moving from Hebrew into Greek, into Latin. This is how the old Canaanite gods and Babylonian kings are being carried into New York City and Washington D.C.—from the far distant past right into the future.

Even so, I am overcome by too much emotion. I am choking on my grief and anger. I am suffocating on my fear. I am overwhelmed by what I have lost and all that I stand to lose. In the face of all the lies, I don't even know what is true anymore. I am tired, exhausted. Spent. My eyes feel too warm. My hands are sweaty. I am missing the connections between it all. A happens, then B, then C, and D. But how did I get there? That's a question that needs an answer.

That's it. That's all I have to say tonight. I have nothing left to confess. There's nothing more I can say to you. And how could I confess to you anyway? But still you lie to me. Why do you lie? Why can't you answer me truthfully? Later on, when all of this is over, you'll recall all the laws, but for now just get out of my sight. Leave me. Get out of here. You're all going to abandon me anyway. Everyone will abandon me. Get out. Get out. I'm tired of looking at you.

[End transcript]

* * *

"It was about this time that DK started having practice raids at the compound, right?"

"Yeah," I tell Myron. "He said that we needed to be ready when they came for us so he had us go through these simulations. Government raids and what not. He'd crank up the air raid siren in the middle of the night and we'd rush to hang up the blackout curtains and to park the pickup trucks and trailers across the entrance to the camp. The little kids and the seniors were moved to the safe room in the middle of the compound 'cause it didn't have any windows. Then he'd use the PA system to play the sound of gunfire, 'To make it authentic,' he said. He called them his Midnight Warnings."

"They must have been loud. The sheriff's office received a number of complaints about your air raid siren and all the gunfire noises and shouting in the early morning hours."

"Yeah?" I didn't know about the complaints. "I didn't think about the neighbors, but I guess that makes sense. It was really loud."

"DK believed that the threat to himself and to Zion's Freedom was imminent," Myron says.

"Yeah. He was pretty worked up about it. Said that the forces of Babylon were coming for us, and that the business of Babylon was our death. He wanted us to be prepared, so everyone took turns keeping watch at the perimeter of the compound and from the watchtower. And we started doing physical training too. Exercises. We built an obstacle course with ropes and tires and a climbing wall and everything. We had to run the obstacle course every day."

"How often did you have these Midnight Warnings?"

"Several times a week. Sometimes they came during the day. Sometimes in the middle of the night. It was random. It wasn't long after the practice raids started that DK made everyone with a job outside the compound quit so they could be part of the training with the rest of us in the compound."

"Was this part of DK's loyalty tests?"

"Yeah, I guess it was. I don't know if he ever called them that."

"What other kinds of tests did he subject you to?"

* * *

[From a transcript of a cassette tape recording of Reverend DK sermon—October 1992]

[Reverend DK] Are you angry? Are you afraid? I know that sometimes those two can feel like the same thing. Frayed nerves. Exhaustion. Irritability. These are the symptoms of both. Sleeplessness. Anxiety, all of it. Your blood pressure goes up and your serotonin levels go down. Anger and fear both take their toll on your physical health as well as your emotional and psychological well-being. You're angry and afraid because you're tired. And you're tired because you're angry and afraid. It's a downward spiral into oblivion. And we're all so afraid of living in oblivion.

Add to all that the effect it has on your spiritual health. We're all being ground down and worn out. We are hard-pressed on every side. We are crushed. We are perplexed. But we haven't begun to despair yet. And that's precisely why I have to demand so much from you. Because we have to be ready. We have to be prepared for what is coming.

If they came in here tonight, if the FBI showed up with tanks and guns and kicked down our doors, would you be ready? What would you be prepared to do? It may be God's will that we should live or that we should die, but either way we will still have to get up and fight against the powers of Babylon, against the forces of evil.

[Murmured remarks from the congregation]

[Reverend DK] Are you willing to do what must be done?

[Shouts from the congregation] Yes! We are! We're ready!

[Reverend DK] Okay. Okay. Quiet now. Carter has a question. Yes, Carter?

[Carter Ahntholz] Should we purchase some more guns before they come for us?

[Reverend DK] How many do we have already?

[Carter Ahntholz] We don't have many. We've got the three AK-47s that you brought back from Texas and a pair of shotguns. And a couple of small caliber handguns. It won't be near enough to stand up against the military forces arrayed against us.

[Reverend DK] No. Thank you, Carter. It will be enough. With God on our side, it will be more than enough.

But put all that aside for now. Don't think about the forces of Babylon. Don't think about the weapons they have prepared for us. And do not be concerned about the precious few weapons we have in our little armory. Put all those fears aside and prepare yourselves instead. Look inward at yourselves and not outward at the enemies that are coming for us. Because, along with fear and anger, there is doubt. And with doubt comes unbelief. You must trust me. If you love God and if you would serve him, you must trust me and do as I say. Without hesitation. Without questions. There won't be time for questions. I need your absolute devotion. Though I am not God—you must think of me as God. I am his authorized agent. I am his appointed commander. And you must be prepared to follow me.

[Applause from the congregation]

[Reverend DK] Would you pick up venomous snakes if I asked you to do it?

[Shouts from the congregation] Yes! Yes!

[Reverend DK] Would you drink poison if I told you it was safe?

[Shouts from the congregation] Yes! You know we would!

[Reverend DK] Would you jump through fire if I said it was necessary?

[Shouts from the congregation] We would! Yes!

[Reverend DK] Would you set yourselves on fire for me?

[Shouts from the congregation] Yes! Yes! Yes!

[Reverend DK] If you are true to me and if you will do as I say—you won't fear anything at all. Not wild animals. Not poisons. Not fire. If you are true to me then there will be nothing that the forces of Babylon can do to hurt you. You will not feel pain any more. We do not fear those who would kill just our bodies. We do not fear them because we know that they cannot touch our souls.

We've been called out into the desert for such a time as this. This is our calling. This is our duty, the duty of love. All those who love the Lord, and all those who love me know the duty of love. We have been called out into the desert and up to this mountain for this particular time. We may not understand all of what is happening, but we are not called to understand. We're called to obey. We train our bodies and prepare our minds so that when the day of testing comes we will be ready to face it. We will not be sleeping. We will be alert and sober.

We have come out into the desert, the mountain, and to the caves because the Babylonian invasion is imminent. And if we have been called out into the desert and up to this mountain with the supplies and provisions that we need, then—when we have gone through the fire and the flames—we will come through on the other side as rulers of the world. Princes and kings. Princess and queens.

Remember the words of the poet who said:

> "But still roll the ancient dead
> and where, oh where have they gone?
> To Babylon. To Babylon."

When you pass through the waters, I will be with you. When you cross rivers, they will not overflow you. When you walk through fire you shall not be burned, neither will the flames take hold of you.

I know the pain that you've endured in this life. I can feel every one of your aches and pains. And I can cure your pain—but only when you believe in me. Only when you trust me. I want you to experience more joy in your lives—this life and the next. I am here to transform you into happier versions of the people that you are now. But you have to listen to me, follow me.

Are you angry? Are you afraid? I know that you are and that's okay. Be angry. I want you to be angry, but in your anger do not sin. And be afraid. I want you to be afraid. But take courage just the same. Are you alert? Are you vigilant? Are you sober? Are you ready to face the forces of Babylon? Are you prepared to do everything I require of you?

[Shouts from the congregation] Yes! Yes! Yes! Yes! Yes!

[End transcript]

CHAPTER NINE

* * *

Maggie stood in the crowded hallway holding her daughter in her arms. Gracie had been crying but her tears were subsiding now. Her eyes were still red and puffy. There were snot bubbles in her nostrils and her breath came in ragged, body convulsing gasps. Maggie patted her on the back and stroked her hair to soothe her. The hallway was loud with echoing conversations and other crying children. Perro, the community's dog, barked and jumped up and down as the people milled past him in the hall.

"Everyone return to your rooms. The danger has passed," DK's disembodied voice came through the PA system cutting through all the other noise. "You did well tonight. You may return to your rooms and rest."

Travis pushed through the hallway, passing the other members of the community as they made their way back to their rooms. He stopped when he saw Maggie and Gracie. "Ms. Snow," he said weakly. "I hoped that I might bump into you before everyone settled for the night."

Maggie smiled limply. "Thanks, Travis. You were really good with the kids tonight. You got them all into the safe room so fast."

"Thanks," he blushed. "Why's Gracie crying? Is she okay? Did she get hurt?"

"She's tired," Maggie said and blew a loose strand of ash-blond hair away from her face. "So am I, honestly. We're all tired, Travis. This is the third Midnight Warning he's called this week."

"Yeah. DK says we're getting better but we're still not fast enough with the trucks and trailers. He says we gotta' get the road blocked before the forces of Babylon can breech the compound. We gotta' get that time down to less than two minutes. It's the most important thing If they get past us there we won't be able to keep them out of the compound."

"Yeah," she sighed. "I get it. But . . . " She paused as she shifted Gracie from one hip to the other. "I know he wants us to be ready, but how ready can we be if everyone is completely exhausted? I was hoping you could maybe say something to DK for us. Especially the kids. They're tired and scared. They need a break. We all need a break." She reached out with one hand, the same hand she'd been using to stroke her daughter's back, and caressed his shoulder. "Please, Travis."

Travis felt warm and flushed. He looked into her eyes. "I could try, but. . . well, you remember what happened to Cornelius. He was removed from the fellowship. I can't challenge him. I wouldn't want to leave . . . I wouldn't want to leave you and Gracie."

Maggie smiled. "I know, Travis. You're very sweet. But he might hear it if it came from you. He trusts you."

"I'll do what I can. I promise."

"Listen," Maggie said as she shifted Gracie's weight again. "DK's told us that he's tired too, right? He'll understand if you tell him that the kids are too tired to keep going like this. He's got to, Travis. He'll listen to you."

"I'll try, Ms. Snow."

Maggie leaned over with the girl on her hip and kissed Travis on the cheek. "Thank you. I thank you and Gracie thanks you." Travis nodded and leaned over to kiss Gracie on the forehead.

"I'll talk to him," Travis promised again. His face was still warm and flushed from her kiss. Just then Perro ran barking through their legs, nearly knocking Travis over. Gracie smiled. Those still in the hallway said goodnight and closed their doors.

* * *

[From a transcript of a cassette tape recording of Reverend DK Bible study—October 1992]

[Reverend DK] We have received by tradition—tradition—that God does not need material offerings. But this is tradition from men and is not completely true. We have been taught and we are convinced, and we do believe that he doesn't need the sacrifice of animals, or grains, or wines poured out on the altar. These kinds of sacrifices are over. They are finished and they are done. And there will be no more of them. Ever. Even the Jews no longer make these sacrifices. They can't. Not anymore. The temple in Jerusalem's been destroyed. There no place for them to make these sacrifices anymore. Now, some of them want to return to that sacrificial system, and there are a surprising number of Evangelical Christians here in America who seem intent on helping the Jews return to those sacrifices. But there will be no more material offerings. Not of these kinds. There will be no more of . . .

[Long pause]

[Chad Lewis] Reverend?

[Reverend DK] . . . [Unintelligible]

[Chad Lewis] Reverend DK, are you okay?

[Reverend DK] Yes. Yes. Sorry. I lost myself for a moment there. But you all know what tomorrow is—it's Halloween. All Hallow's Eve. The night when kids get dressed up as ghouls and ghosts and other agents of darkness to beg for candy and to vandalize homes and to destroy property. It's an evil night. But this isn't something that makes me angry. Not with the kids anyway. They're being led astray by adults who should know better. They're being taught that this is acceptable by their parents—many of whom are ignorant themselves because their parents taught the same. It goes back generations.

But who's really at fault here? Who is the real enemy? Who is killing the children? The police? The KKK? With or without help from the police? Is it an international conspiracy of Satanists? There are hundreds of satanic covens across this country and they're abducting children for their Luciferian rituals. They are feeding the flesh of children to the politicians. Are they the enemy? Or is it the Knights Templar? Is it the Brotherhood of Games? No one remembers the Brotherhood of Games anymore. But I do. I saw what they did in Europe during the Middle Ages. But who is killing the children these days? The FBI? The CIA? The World Health Organization? The CDC? The Center for Disease Control is abducting and murdering little black boys to harvest adrenochrome from their penises in order to live forever.

[Long pause]

[Chad Lewis] Reverend? You're scaring us. What's happening?

[Reverend DK] There are children buried in the foundations of the London Bridge. That's what the nursery rhyme is about. [Singing] London Bridge is falling down, falling down, falling down. . . They believed that a bridge would collapse without a human sacrifice buried into its foundations. We could go over to Lake Haversu, that's where the London Bridge is today. We could go out to Lake Haversu and find those murdered children, but you have to ask yourself, who is killing the children?

[Chad Lewis] Reverend! Please. . .

[Reverend DK] All right! Everyone go to bed. Leave me alone. I'm done. Go away!

[End transcript]

* * *

Working late into the afternoon, DK, Travis, and a number of the other men of Zion's Freedom labored to put up a barbed wire fence around the boundary of their property. This late in the year, the temperatures in the desert didn't get much over seventy degrees, even late in the afternoon. During the night temperatures would drop down to the fifties. The men worked hard and sweated, but they were not overheated. The fence-line that they constructed stretched a semicircle around the front of their compound of mobile homes and trailers with a swinging gate at the main road. Behind the buildings was the cliff face of the mountain. The men dug holes for fence posts and poured concrete to set them firmly in place. And, wearing thick leather gloves to protect their hands, they strung the posts with coiled lengths of sharp barbed wire.

As they worked, DK told them of his memories of the rebel fortress at Masada. "We didn't have barbed wire like this, of course, but we were secured at the top of a mountain fortress. It had been built in the classic style of the early Roman Empire by Herod the Great. He was mad, of course. Paranoid that everyone was out to get him. And why wouldn't they be? Right? I mean he killed anyone who got too close to him, or anyone he thought was a threat to his position. Even members of his own family—especially members of his own family!"

He paused to remove his gloves and wiped the sweat and dirt from his face. Then he took a long drink of water from the jug they kept along with their supplies on the back of one of the compound's pickup trucks. "We had water, but it wasn't cold like this. It was kept in large cisterns. I'll tell you this much—Herod the Great might have been a mad, murderous bastard, but he was also a genius. Or at least knew how to hire geniuses for his building projects. The water system of Masada could collect enough water from a single day's worth of rain to keep a thousand people hydrated for over two years. When Herod built, he built big. It was a lavish place for him and his entourage along with all their families, servants, and guards."

The others listened as they worked. Travis hauled another coil of wire from the back of the pickup truck. A couple of the men leaned on their shovels as they listened to their leader's memories.

"I studied Middle Eastern history under the late Professor Ernesto Gutierrez at the University of Akron," DK told them. "Go Zips! He was a wonderful man and a great instructor, but he was wrong. He tried to tell us that there is no archaeological evidence to support the only historical record of our final stand and our deaths at that mountain top fortress. He said that Flavius Josephus, who chronicled the mass suicide of our rebel band, fabricated the whole event. He said that there was no archaeological evidence at all of any battle ever being fought there outside of Josephus' writings. I tried to tell him the truth about it, but Professor Gutierrez, as brilliant as he was, he wouldn't listen to me."

DK paused again to put his leather gloves back on and to pick up the next bundle of barbed wire. "I told Professor Gutierrez that absence of evidence is not evidence of absence, but he ignored me. He told the class that what evidence there is at the site is limited and cannot clearly corroborate the historicity of Josephus' account. And, that given Josephus' other inaccuracies and his tendency to exaggerate and to inflate, and even to create events, should give us pause when there is no other supporting evidence."

DK stopped and laughed. "But Professor Gutierrez wasn't there, was he? Not like I was. I still remember the words of our leader, Eleazar Ben-Yair. He said, 'At this crisis let us not disgrace ourselves. We've refused to submit even to a slavery that would involve no peril, so we won't now, along with slavery, deliberately accept the irreparable penalties waiting for us if we are captured by Roman hands. We were the first of all to revolt against them. So we will be the last in arms against them. Moreover, I believe it is God who has granted us this favor so that we have it in our power to die nobly and in freedom.' His very words. I remember them clearly. Eleazar Ben-Yair was a brave man and I respected him. We all respected him and followed him without question or hesitation. That's how nine hundred and sixty of us took our own lives. Men, women, and children. We surrendered our lives to each other and to God rather than surrender them to the Romans."

John Hawkins, who had been working and sweating there along with the other men, looked up, puzzled. "I thought you told us you'd studied at the University of Minnesota."

DK sighed and dropped the wire he'd been rolling out. "I took a number of classes at both universities, John. I studied at a lot of places, okay. I've been a student everywhere I've gone, learning from anyone and everyone I ever met. I've learned something from every book I've ever read. And I've read thousands of them. Ten thousand books, maybe. I am a student of the world, John Hawkins. You can't stop knowledge."

"Okay. Okay. Okay," John said timidly. "I'm sorry. I didn't mean nothing. I was just confused. I mean, you've had all these experiences, been all these places, in this life and in your other lives. Sometimes it just gets difficult to keep them all straight."

"Well, I don't know what to tell you," DK said with a light lipped frown. "You're just going to have to pay closer attention, I guess. I can't help it if you aren't listening closely and if you get confused. I can't hold your hand and walk you through all of this, you know. You're just going to have to keep up."

"Yes, DK."

"Do you understand?"

"Yes, DK."

"You said once that you believed that I am a prophet. Is that still true, John Hawkins? Do you still believe that I am a prophet of the Lord?"

"Yes, DK. Of course I believe. You are the prophet of the Lord."

"What happens to people who challenge or otherwise question the prophets, John?"

"DK . . ."

"What happens to them? They are struck blind or dead, right? They get eaten by bears, right? Or burnt up in fires falling from heaven, isn't that right?"

"Yes, DK."

"Touch not the Lord's anointed, John. Touch not the Lord's anointed. That's a fair warning for you to keep in mind. Do you remember what to happened to Jimmy Wolf?"

"Yes, DK," John said. "I remember. We all remember."

"Good. Good. Now, I don't know for certain that Jimmy Wolf's heart attack wouldn't have happened anyway—even if he hadn't challenged me that night—he was pretty old, after all, but do you really want to take that kind of risk, John Hawkins? Do you?"

"No, DK."

"And whether I was studying at the University of Minnesota or at the University of Akron isn't really the point of the story is it John?"

"No, DK. I suppose it's not."

"I was trying to tell you some of what I remember of Masada."

"Yes, DK."

"Good. Good. Now I want the rest of you to go on back to the hall DK said to the other men "Go back and wash up. John Hawkins is going to finish this fence-line before he rejoins the group for dinner."

The men nodded their understanding and stripped off their work gloves and put their shovels in the back of the pickup truck. After the last of them had walked away, DK stared at John Hawkins, stripped off his own gloves and walked away leaving Hawkins to finish hanging the final stretch of wire alone. He worked for the next several hours, sweating into the chill evening. When he finally finished the fence and returned all the tools and supplies to the storage shed and when he had parked the pickup truck alongside the other Zion's Freedom vehicles, he went in to take a shower. He'd missed dinner so he went in to the evening Bible study still tired and hungry.

* * *

"Hey, Myron," I call out.

"Yeah, Travis?"

"How did you get copies of DK's sermon tapes? I thought everything like that was destroyed when the compound burned down."

"It was. There was little to be salvaged from the ruins of the Zion's Freedom compound, but DK recorded just about every sermon and Bible study session he had with the folks there. He recorded several of his songs as well, but there was very little of any of it that remained in the compound after the fire. We got lucky with these recordings. One of the Zion's Freedom folks, Gloria Reynolds, had a sister in Des Moines, Iowa. She sent her copies of some of DK's recordings—the sermons, and Bible studies, and worship songs, hoping that perhaps her sister would come out to Arizona to join her. We got the tapes from her. She told us that Gloria had nearly convinced her to move out to Arizona, but that her husband was dead set against it and wouldn't let her go."

"Oh," I say. "I remember Ms. Gloria. She was always going on about how everyone around the world needed to hear DK's message. She sometimes went door to door trying to tell people about DK. Sometimes DK had to tell her to knock it off, but she just wouldn't stop. She was a nice old lady, though. A little weird maybe. And she had bad teeth. Like her teeth were crossed. She was nice but she looked weird when she smiled. And she was almost always smiling."

"Is that so?"

"Yeah. I guess it makes sense. Ms Gloria wanted everyone to join us at Zion's Freedom. Maybe it's a good thing that her sister never came out to be with her—with us. What with the fires and all . . . "

"Yeah," Myron agrees. "It certainly turned out to be a good thing for her."

Chapter Ten

"WE'VE COME TO THE part of the story that has garnered the most attention from the media—the raid, the stand-off, the deaths, the fire. But there are still a number of important questions that I need to ask you. We still want to understand what happened from an insider's perspective. We have the video recordings from the news crews that were there on the scene and we have recordings made by the police and the FBI during negotiations with DK and with you. But we don't have anything from inside the compound. What I want is to see what happened in those last days through your eyes, Travis."

"I understand." Myron is very kind.

"Are you ready to continue?" he asks me. I tell him that I am.

"It isn't entirely clear what the initial instigating event was. It seems that a postal carrier named Bradford Johnstone attempted to deliver a piece of certified mail to the compound, one that required a signature from the recipient and that someone in the compound—possibly DK himself—mistook him for an agent of Babylon and shot him in the stomach."

"That sounds right," I say. I wasn't there, but it sounds like what could have happened.

"Fortunately carrier Johnstone didn't die of his injuries. But he might have. He might have died right there on the driveway to Zion's Freedom if one of the members of the community had not called 911. They saved his life. Do you know who it was that called for the ambulance?"

"No. Like I said, I wasn't there when everything started going down. The whole place was already in chaos when I got back. It was all confusing. So much was happening all at once."

"We have a recording of the 911 call. We can play it for you," Myron says and he has Dave play it for me.

[Transcript 911 call]

[911 Operator] Superior Police, what's the address of the emergency?

[Unidentified Voice] There's a postman here. He's been shot. I think he's dying. Please send help.

[911 Operator] Okay. What's the address? Where are you?

[Long pause]

[911 Operator] Sir? What's the address of the emergency? Where . . .

[Unidentified Voice] We're at the Zion's Freedom compound out the end of Ridge Road.

[911 Operator] And what is the phone number you're calling from?

[Unidentified Voice] I . . . I can't . . . give you that. I . . .

[911 Operator] Emergency responders have been dispatched to your location, sir. Please stay on the line.

[Call disconnects]

[End transcript]

"I know the quality of the recording isn't great, but do you recognize the voice of the caller? Can you identify the individual who called 911 to save carrier Johnstone?"

"It sounds like Hawkins," I tell him.

"That would be John Hawkins?" Myron asks.

"Yeah. It sounds like John, but I'm not sure."

"It was also never determined who actually shot Bradford Johnstone. Do you know who pulled the trigger, Travis? Was it the Reverend?"

"I don't know," I tell him again. "I wasn't there when it happened."

"But . . . "

"I wasn't there."

* * *

Travis peddled his bike up the hill that lead to the compound he'd called home for the last six months. In that time he'd found a familial love that he'd never known, either from his absent father or his unenergetic mother. The members of Zion's Freedom had welcomed him from the first. They'd loved him as one of their own. And he'd warmed to their demonstrations of affection, taking pride in them just as they'd been proud of him. He belonged. He was one of them.

On this particular day Travis had gone into town to do a small bit of shopping. He wasn't old enough to ride DK's motorcycle on his own so he'd taken his old BMX bike. It had been blue and red when it was shiny new, but now most of the paint and shine had been scuffed and scraped away. He'd ridden his bike into town in order to buy a birthday gift for little Gracie Snow—who he'd come to think of as his own kid sister.

* * *

I'd thought about getting her this cool looking stuffed animal—a snake. It was black and green and had these glittery scales. It was pretty and not scary at all. It looked really cool. But I didn't get it because I didn't want little Gracie to think she could pick up the real snakes that we saw around the compound and play with them the way that she could play with her stuffed animal. So I got her a stuffed armadillo instead. It was purple and pink. I think she would have liked it."

"That was considerate of you," Myron tells me. "Thoughtful."

"And I bought it for her with my own money. Before joining Zion's Freedom, I probably would have just shoplifted it. I could snatched it out of the store without anyone knowing but I picked it out and bought it myself. It meant more that way. It was honest. It was true."

"That's nice, Travis. It's clear that you really cared for her."

* * *

The last hill coming from town up the Zion's Freedom compound was steep enough that Travis had to stand on the pedals of his bike to get enough push to keep his forward momentum. He was huffing and wheezing when he peddled past the pickup trucks parked near the front gates, ready to barricade the entrance at a moment's notice. That's where he saw the familiar, box shaped delivery truck parked just outside the compound's gates. He looked in the window of the truck as he cruised by, but the mailman wasn't in inside.

Several members of the compound were gathered in front of the main building which was covered with signs—hand lettered with Bible verses. "Now is the day of Salvation," and "Clothe yourself in strength, O Zion." The largest, mounted above the front door, proclaimed in a bold script painted in a vibrant pink paint, "Fear NOT, Daughter of ZION; your KING is Coming!" Travis dropped his bike in the gravel driveway and ran the last few yards to the cluster of people. "What's going on? He called out and then he saw what they'd been staring at.

The mailman who'd parked his truck just outside the compound was laying face down in the gravel, bleeding from a gunshot wound in his stomach. He satchel was under his body. When he'd fallen he'd landed on it and crushed a box labeled with a sticker—"LIVE CRICKETS"—that he'd been carrying. Now the crickets were escaping and jumping and crawling across his body. One jumped into the corner of his eye. Another was attempting to crawl into his nostril. They chirruped on and around his body.

∗ ∗ ∗

"The crickets were probably for the Lamont's pet lizard, Sheila. They had them delivered every couple of weeks."

"A pet iguana?" Myron asks from where he is sitting behind the lights.

"No. Not an iguana. Sheila was a Blue tongued Skink. Gideon said that they're from Australia Sheila was cool. Gideon and Janice let me feed her and hold her sometimes."

"Nip. Perro. Sheila . . . The members of Zion's Freedom had an affinity for funny pet names, didn't they?"

I don't understand Myron's comment. He explains that Sheila is slang for a girl in Australia. I didn't know that. I guess it is sorta' funny. I wonder what other jokes the adults at Zion's Freedom had that I missed while I was with them.

"So postal carrier Johnstone had two deliveries for the Lamonts that day." Myron says this as if it was something he'd already known.

"Other than junk mail, the Lamonts were the only ones to get real mail at the compound," I say. "Except Ms. Gloria, I guess. She got a few letters from her sister. Everyone else just said that there was no one on the outside that they needed to talk to."

"The certified letter Johnstone carried to the compound that day was for the Lamonts. It was some legal documents concerning the sale of of one of their properties in Sedona. It seems that they'd sold one of their houses and were preparing to donate the proceeds of the sale to Reverend DK."

∗ ∗ ∗

"Is he dead? Should we do something for him," Travis said as he pushed past the others who were standing there.

"Travis . . . " one of them said. It was Claudia Kemper. She was holding her five year old daughter, Lilly, to her chest. "Don't . . . "

"But he's hurt. He's bleeding. We should . . . " Travis didn't have any idea what they should do next. He trusted the adults to know. Just then they began hearing police sirens in the distance. And then, much closer, they heard the air-raid siren wailing within the compound.

"Oh, it's another of his damned Midnight Warnings!" hissed Carol Hendrickson.

"Are you kidding, Carol?" Claudia scolded. "Look what's happened and use your brains. This is for real. This it it! It's really happening. All of it, just like DK told us."

DK's voice came over the PA system just then. "They're coming for us, my beloved. This is what I've been warning you about. They're coming for us. Everyone to your emergency stations. Run. Run. They're coming. Run."

The gathered members of the compound began running for their emergency stations. Travis stripped the backpack he carried from his back and flung it to the ground and began running for the daycare room to make sure the children were in their safety locations. Then he would help hang the blackout curtains in front of the windows. The purple and pink stuffed armadillo he'd purchased for Gracie was forgotten inside the backpack.

* * *

"It was shortly after that, only a few minutes, that police and ambulance crews arrived—responding to the 911 call from the compound. And maybe half an hour after that, the FBI agents arrived as well. It all happened fast."

"That's pretty much how I remember it—but I was really busy getting the kids into their safe room and putting up the blackout curtains, so I didn't actually see them arrive. I saw them from the watchtower later, circled outside our property line. I saw the paramedics carrying the mailman out on one those rolling stretchers to put him in the ambulance. They had to lift him over the back of the pickup trucks to get him out. And I thought I recognized the FBI agents when they got there."

"Yeah. It was agents Marcus and Ramirez again, the same agents who came to question DK about Marla Glenn. They were the first. Other agents arrived later as the incident went on, but agents Marcus and Ramirez were the first federal agents on the scene. You spoke to agent Ramirez on the phone a number of times."

"I remember talking to him—on the phone and outside the buildings. But I couldn't remember his name. It's been a long time."

"What do you remember?" Myron asks me.

"I remember the shouting, mostly. And the crying. People were shouting questions and DK was shouting orders. Everyone was running up and down the halls, making sure the doors were locked and barricaded and that the windows were covered. The little ones were crying because they were scared. They didn't know what was happening. Not yet. And none of us knew what to do. Except DK. He knew exactly how to take control of the situation."

* * *

"Oh, thank heaven," Marie Mason said. She'd pulled back a corner of the blackout curtain and was watching the activity outside. "He's not dead. He's still alive, praise God. I think he's he's moving."

"The paramedic team in the driveway loaded the now bandaged postal carrier onto a gurney and wheeled him to the ambulance with deliberate haste. The bullet wound in his stomach was still bleeding. Marie could see the blood stain on his uniform as they lifted the gurney into the back of the ambulance and drove away with lights flashing and siren blaring.

"I want to look," Travis said as he poked his head through the curtain to see what was going on. The lights and sirens flared as the ambulance roared to life and rolled down the driveway away from the compound. The emergency vehicle nearly collided with a gray sedan pulling up to the gates.

"Travis," a voice boomed behind him and he jumped. He dropped the blackout curtain and stood up straight in the hallway in front of DK. "I'm going to need you to do something for me," DK told him and smiled.

"Yes, DK. I'll do anything."

"I need you to go outside and speak to the police and the FBI agents that are setting themselves up against us out there. I want you to give them a message from me." Travis gaped at DK. "Don't worry. They haven't organized themselves yet. They have even less of an idea of what's going on here than we do. They'll still be waiting for someone to take charge and tell them what to do."

"Okay, DK." Travis said. "What do you want me to tell them?"

"I want you to go out the front doors and tell the FBI agents who just arrived that we are a peaceable community of religious individuals—men, women, and children. Be sure to tell them that there are children here. Also make sure that they understand that we have a number of guns here and that law enforcement cannot enter here without a legal warrant."

"What if they won't listen to me?"

"They will. They don't have a plan yet. They're going to be arguing about who has jurisdiction for a while yet, so they'll listen to you. They don't know who else to listen to yet. You'll be in charge of the situation. You're my man, Travis. Just as I am the Silence of God, you will be my voice to those outside."

Travis took several deep breaths, then nodded and proceeded to the front doors. He raised his hands above his head and, when DK opened the doors, stepped though slowly. Then the doors closed behind him and he was alone with the enemy. Immediately the police officers and FBI agents milling about in front of the compound drew their weapons and trained them on Travis. He stopped and stood still to address them.

"I need to speak to the FBI agent in charge, he said as loudly as he could without actually shouting. "Who's in charge here, please?"

"I guess that would be me," said one of the two nearly indistinguishable FBI agents. "At least until we get a trained hostage negotiator down here."

"Then I guess I should be speaking to you, sir," Travis said. "I've been told that I should tell you that we have no hostages here. No one is being held at gunpoint. No one is here against their will. We're all here because we want to be. We're not terrorists. We are a peaceable community of religious individuals—men, women, and children. We don't want anyone else to get hurt."

"Neither do we, son. Neither do we," the agent interrupted. "None of us here wants to see this collapse into violence. We want to make sure that everyone gets out of this safe and unharmed—everyone. Your people and ours. I promise you that."

Travis continued unfazed by the interruption. "But I've also been told to warn you that we are armed. We don't want anyone to get hurt, but we do have guns and we can shoot. Also I'm supposed to say that we can't let any of you in without a legal and proper warrant."

"What's your name, son?" the FBI agent called out.

"Travis, sir. Travis Thompson Took. Some people call me Triple-T."

"Thank you, Travis. How many of you are there in this peaceable community of religious individuals?"

Travis shook his head. "That's all I've got to tell you right now. I might be given more to say later, but that's all I can tell you right now." He stepped backwards, his arms still raised, and knocked at the door. Marie Mason opened it and, when Travis stepped through, quickly closed it again. Travis looked around but DK was no where to be seen.

"Leave him alone, Travis. He's gone into his room to pray," Marie Mason said demurely. "Don't worry. He'll come back to us when he's heard from the Lord. Don't worry."

* * *

"It was hard to wait for him. It seemed like he was in his room forever. He was in his room praying while our home was being surrounded by police cars and FBI agents. He was still there a couple of hours later when the SWAT van from Phoenix arrived. They set up a police line at the edge of the driveway. We were trapped inside."

"What do you do while you were waiting?"

"Some people were praying. Someone was in the chapel singing—I don't know who it was. Carter Ahntholz opened up the gun cabinet and started loading all the guns with ammo. His wife, Joan, was in the kitchen cooking. I don't know what she was making, but I remember that it smelled terrible."

"But what did you do, Travis?"

"I sat with the kids for a while. Mostly to make sure that Gracie was okay. But she wasn't scared at all. Some of the other kids were crying—mostly, I think, because some of the adults were crying. They did what they saw us doing. But Gracie, she just played with her toys and laughed like nothing was going on. After a while, I went to my room to find something."

"What was it," Myron asks but I don't answer. Instead I ask him a question.

"Can I ask you a question?"

"Sure. Go ahead."

"You said you was an author. How many books have you written?"

"I've published four books about true crime and one historical novel about the Ludlow Massacre under the pseudonym Matthew Havel."

"Pseudonym? That's like a pen name, right?"

"Exactly, Travis."

"I wrote something once. Do you want to hear it?"

"Absolutely. What is it?"

"I wrote a poem for Ms. Snow, but I never got a chance to share it with her. That's what I went to find in my room. I had it hidden under my bunk. But I didn't get a chance to give it to her. Things went bad before I could."

"Do you still have a copy of it?"

"No. But I've got it memorized. It's the only thing I ever wrote."

"I would love to hear your poem, Travis," Myron says. So I recite the poem for him. The whole thing, word for word, just as I wrote it for her:

> In winter's chill, what is it that I behold?
> A woman as beautiful as snow, and cold.
> Her skin as fair as purest white,
> She's a beauty, oh what a sight.
>
> Her eyes, like jewels, they sparkle and they gleam,
> she is so enchanting, just like a dream.
> Her eyes hold secrets and stories untold,
> like whispers of winter, icy, cold.
>
> Her smile, like the moon up in the sky
> bringing warmth to the coldest hearts nearby.
> A beacon of light in the darkest of nights
> melting away my worries and my chilling frights.
>
> Her face, like a snowflake's grace
> leaves a mark that cannot be erased.
> Her beauty, like a winter's landscape so rare,
> fills my heart with wonder, beyond compare.
>
> Oh, Oh lady fair, as beautiful as snow,
> your elegance forever glows.
> A charming figure of winter's embrace
> full of beauty, full of grace.

Myron is quiet as he listens and says nothing when I finish. I am afraid that he thinks it was stupid. I begin to think that I shouldn't have shared it with him. It was stupid. But instead he says, "Thank you, Travis. That was very nice. It's too bad that you were unable to share it with Ms. Snow. I'm sure she would have appreciated it."

* * *

DK found Travis rushing through the hallway. "Triple-T, just the man I wanted to see. Come with me, Travis."

"But I was going to get something . . . "

"Can it wait?" DK asked. "We're in a terrible fix here, Travis."

"Yeah," Travis sighed. "It can wait. I'll get it later."

"Good. Good," DK said. "Because I need you to take another message to the FBI outside."

Travis nodded slowly. It seemed that at that moment the hallway was suddenly empty. The people milling about, moving back and forth among the rooms of the connected trailers moving furniture, carrying boxes, or children, or hammering boards over windows, were suddenly gone. Their noise was replaced with silence.

"I would go myself," DK told the boy, "but I have been instructed by the Lord to remain still. I am to remain at rest. At least for now. Perhaps I will have something more to do later, but my role for now is to remain silent. Instead you are to speak for me."

Travis gave him a nervous smile and said, "Sure, DK. What do you want me to say?"

"Read this." DK handed him a sheet of notebook paper that had been torn from a spiral binder. Handwritten on the lines in a tight scribble was a message from DK to the authorities outside. It took Travis several moments to puzzle out some of the words. He read it through three times while the Reverend DK waited in silence.

"We will not be assimilated. We will not be integrated. We will not be fused with others. Defeat and annihilation are immanent. So we must escape. We must escape the world because the world cannot be purified and we would be pure. We must keep ourselves from the contamination of the world. The world is burning. It can do no other. The earth was born to burn and it will burn forever, and the smoke of its torment will rise forever and ever. This is why we choose to burn briefly now rather than burn forever later."

"For years now the Humanists, Communists, Zionists, Modernists, and Mythicists have been taking over, not only in the U.S. government, but they've also been infiltrating the leadership of American churches. And what is worse is that they are working in conjunction with the Antichrist, preparing the way for him in the wilderness of these times with their systematic depravations. And the coming of the Great King of Terror in the sky—the coming of the comet is his dreadful sign. So it is better to die pure than to live corrupted. Now there is a new comet which is, in fact, a very old comet—an exotic, green comet not seen in the skies over our heads since the Stone Age when our primitive ancestors were living in caves and warring with the Neanderthals. This comet hasn't been seen in our skies for nearly fifty thousand years. Now the King of Terrors returns and there is little time. Make your arrangements with God."

"I don't get it. What's all this about a comet?" Travis asked looking up from the sheet of notebook paper.

"Misdirection," DK said with a gleam in his eye and a grin on his lips as he smoothed down a mess of wild hair. "It's a bit of heavenly deception, if you will, to confuse them. It's okay to lie if it's to benefit the community. It's like the Egyptian midwives lying to the Pharaoh. And it's not lying, is it? Not really. Think of it as a simple misdirection that will give us more time to do the things we need to do before the end."

"But. . ."

"Think of it as a game. It's our game to win. And we can change the rules when we need to, Travis. This is the lightning round at the end of the world. This is sudden death. So just take that message out there and read it for them. Everything will be fine."

Outside, in the glare of the police floodlights, Travis read from the prepared statement. "Cut the crap, kid," The FBI agent said through an electronic bullhorn. "We're not here about your religious convictions. We're here because someone in your peaceable religious community shot Bradford Johnstone and because your leader, Lewis Earl Howard, also known as Sixten Everett Johnson—I think you guys call him Reverend DK—is wanted in connection to a murder of a sixteen year old girl in Indiana in 1981. Don't make this a religious persecution deal. You could be worshiping a two-headed cow from the planet Venus, and I wouldn't give a fig. This isn't about doctrine or religious dogma. It's about crime, kid. That's all."

Travis stared blankly into the lights pointed at him fro the police line at the edge of the property. Frozen and disoriented. Then he turned and fled back inside the compound.

"Why did DK have you act as his intermediary with the FBI? Why didn't he speak to them himself?"

This is something I've thought about all these years but I still really don't know. DK had his own ways and plans. He knew his own mind, even if no one else did. "He was studying and praying. And he was making his final recording—which he had me give to the FBI." That's all I know to say.

"The so-called DK Basement Tape," Myron says. "That's what the media called it at the time."

"Yeah. The Basement Tape, but I don't know why everyone calls it that. We didn't even have a basement at the compound."

"That was the VHS taped communique that you delivered to the FBI, correct?"

"Yeah. I carried it out to them. I thought for sure that they were going to shoot me or grab me and put a hood over my head and throw me in the back of their car. But I handed them the videotape and turned around and walked back to the building without saying a word—and they didn't do anything to me."

∗∗∗

The members of Zion's Freedom spent a restless night in the compound, surrounded by the members of the Superior police department as well as police officers from Phoenix and officers from the Pinal County Sheriff's Department and a handful of FBI agents. The officers cordoned off a semi-circle in front of the compound, effectively besieging the community, trapping them between the law enforcement line and the rock wall of the Superstition Mountains. A rueful gust of wind rattled loose sheets of aluminum and vinyl siding along the sides of the trailers. Somewhere in the dark a mountain lion screamed like a wounded woman.

The police kept their diesel generator powered spot lights trained on the front of the compound buildings. Watching and waiting. They were there to prevent anyone from making an escape—no way in, no way out. Except through them. Members of DK's community kept their own guard inside through the night, taking shifts in the watchtower—watching for police movement and activity.

Parents of the Zion's Freedom children laid on the floor next to their little ones, stroking their back and gently brushing their hair to keep them calm. Few of them slept—and those who did, slept fitfully, tossing, turning, and waking every few hours in a confused state. Marie Mason spent the night in the chapel on her knees, praying for deliverance. Others joined her for an hour or two at a time, keeping a twenty-four hour prayer vigil, each of them praying that the Lord of Hosts would come to their immediate aid.

DK, working in the Bible study lecture room, recorded his final taped communique for the police and the FBI. Travis helped by setting up the lights and operating the camera. John Hawkins, Carter Ahntholz, and Goyathlay Hernandez took shifts, patrolling the hallways with loaded firearms. They checked and rechecked that the doors were locked and barricaded and that the winders were locked and covered with the blackout curtains.

When dawn came it came not as a relief or a break in the tension. There would be no relief in that new morning's light. The sun rose over them like a threat. The sun rose with a promise of blood and of violence.

* * *

[From a transcript of the video recorded communique from Reverend DK delivered to the FBI by Travis Took. The Reverend DK is seated on a three-legged stool in front of a white board. He is dressed in cowboy boots, blue jeans, a plain white t-shirt, and a black leather vest. He is also wearing large, dark sunglasses]

[Reverend DK] To the various members of Arizona law enforcement, and members of the Federal Bureau of Investigation, and to the reporters and journalists of the news media, and to the world at large: Good afternoon. I am the Reverend DK, leader of Zion's Freedom in Superior, Arizona, now surrounded and besieged by the forces of a hostile government.

We are trapped here in our own home—men, women, and children who have done nothing to hurt or harm anyone else. We are surrounded by violent men who would cruelly and illegally take us away by force. We are surrounded by forces that wish to destroy us completely.

I do not understand this abyss. I do not understand how it is that we have come to this. I do not understand the absurd absence of love and divine light that has led us to this point. But, and this is important, it is not necessary for me to understand. Here is a bridge to be crossed, a bridge stretching out over empty nothingness. And we will cross it. There is nothing else to understand. Nothing else to be done.

Now, I am not a violent man, ordinarily, in my own life. Understand me? I have no violence in me. I am a brand plucked out of the fire in the face of an everlasting darkness. But these are not ordinary times and this is not just about me. This is about all of us who have made this place our home. We did not ask for this violence. We did not seek it out. We came to this place in the desert to make a quiet and peaceable home with our friends and our families. We came to this place to live in the light of God, but we have been plunged into darkness. You have thrust us into the dark of night.

You come to us now and you invade our property. You surround us with rifles and guns yet you talk about law and order. You stand ready to kick in our doors yet you talk about peace. You are prepared to steal our children and yet you talk about dignity and human rights. And we are tired of your hypocrisy.

We are ready to take risks and we are ready to die. Ready to bleed and to die. If that's what it takes—then that's what we'll do. And we're good at it. Some of us have done this before. Many times before. We have lived and we have died. We've been through all this before. And we're more than ready to die again if that is our fate. There's more to it, of course, and our message could bring you peace but you won't hear it. Not from us. You refuse to listen to us.

We will lay down our lives in peace, like barefooted servants in the house of the great king. Peaceably and on our own terms. Not because you come at us with guns and with violence and hatred. We lay down our lives because we no longer need this life. We are ready. We are prepared to move into the next life. Death is preferable to the endless agonies of this life.

You might say that we are dangerous. You might say that we are irrational. You will probably say that we are insane. But we expected this kind of reaction. We anticipated your hostility. What else could you do. You are who you are and we are who we are. That is why we came out to this place—to get away. To hide ourselves away from your aggressions. But here you are, pounding on our doors, banging away as if to shake the dead. You came to us. Remember that. You pursued us. We did not start this. But we knew it would come to this. Still we cannot help but to be disappointed. The world is a weary place and we are tired. So very tired.

Soon this will all be over. Soon we will leave this place. We will be gone and you will remain. But this is only a semblance of the true reality. For it is we who will remain after the fires have been quenched and the ashes blown away. We will remain forever in the presence of the one true God. And when we have taken leave from this place we shall cite the value of silence and praise the mouth of darkness. Let all those who want to live, live. Those who do not want to fight in this world of eternal, glorified struggle are not destined to live.

Now, as to the suspicions that you are bringing against me—suspicions and accusations of violence and murder—I can only say this: you have no proof. You've dredged up an old, forgotten name, Lewis Earl Howard, and you think this name is mine. You think that you know something about me. But you don't. You don't know anything about me or my mission in this time and place.

You want to ask me about this girl, Marla. But you cannot say that I knew her or even that Lewis Earl Howard, whoever he might have been, knew her. You have suspicions. You have questions. But you do not know the truth of things. And this is unfortunate—for the truth, if you knew it, would set you free. Free from all of your suspicions and free from all of your questions.

Marla is dead. Her precious life was cut short and this causes me a measure of sadness. All death causes me a measure of grief. All death wounds and grieve me. I have lived my entire life under the shadow of death, and I continually feel the weight of its shadow hanging over me. But I can do nothing about her death. I can offer no comfort for her loss except that small comfort that is offered to all of us. And that comfort is to know that death is not the end. There is life and there is death. And there is life after death. And there is life after life. I think of this always.

But I won't talk about her death. What could I say about it? What could I say except to tell you this: the police investigating her death disguised themselves as neighborhood toughs and spent hours chasing down false reports and dead end leads, hoping to get lucky. But nothing happened. Nothing came of it. Call it insufficient effort. Call it indifferent follow through. Blame it on their mistakes and failures. Blame it on a lack of warrant. They were cutting corners while the real killer was cutting something—or someone - else. And here you are now, chasing ghosts that don't even look like me. The pictures you've formed in your minds don't look like me at all.

I am grieved and wounded and wasted. But I will return. I always return. Again and again and again with my pain. The life that I live, the life within me, never dies. And neither does the pain, for all of life is pain. The bells may be broken, but they still ring. My heart might be broken, but it still beats. I shall be grieved, and I shall die, but I shall return. I never really leave. All around me I can hear the sound of the empire falling, broken into shattered fragments. The clock is ticking and the world is burning. We are choking on smoke and fumes. But this will all soon be over.

The rest is up to you. And one way or another, it will all be over. That's all I can tell you, except this one last thing: You're going to miss me when I'm gone.

[Reverend DK smiles, then stands up from his stool. He walks toward the camera and turns it off]

[End transcript]

* * *

"Those final messages—the hand written note and the videotaped statement that you delivered to the FBI—really confused them," Myron tells me. "If DK's intent was to create confusion and to stir up dissent among the agents and officers outside the compound, he certainly succeeded. There was no consensus among them about how to proceed. Some wanted to gear up with rifles, and body armor, and flashbangs to storm the compound immediately. They wanted to bring in an armored personnel carrier from the Arizona National Guard and send it crashing through the front doors so that they could breech the compound and take the place by force. Others argued that they needed to wait DK out. They argued that you couldn't have enough supplies to hold out for too long and that an end to the crisis could be achieved without resorting to violence and inevitable death. The law enforcement agents outside your compound divided into two arguing camps and there was no clear chain of command to give leadership. They were still arguing about what to do when the fires started."

"I guess we were confused inside the compound too," I say.

"How so?"

"There were some who wanted to surrender and leave the compound. They said that we hadn't broken any laws and that if we gave ourselves up the whole thing could be sorted out before anyone got hurt. The ones with children said that this was the best way to makes sure that the kids would be safe. Others said that, of course we hadn't done anything wrong and that the police had no right to surround our home. They wanted to stay and to fight, if it came to that. Others said that we should just trust DK to tell us what to do. There was a lot of argument about it at first but we decided to wait and to trust DK. Everyone trusted that he had a plan and that we were going to follow his plan."

"And that's how it played out, isn't it? No matter what the police and the FBI outside would have decided, and no matter what the individual members of Zion's Freedom may have wanted to do, DK had his own end-game in mind, didn't he?"

"Yeah, I guess he did."

Chapter Eleven

DK came out of his private rooms and summoned everyone to the Bible study hall where he could share with them the conclusions he'd reached during his time of contemplation. Weary and nervous members of the community made their way to the hall. Their eyes were red and puffy from lack of sleep. Their hair was greasy and uncombed. They carried listless children in their arms. The littlest ones sucked their thumbs. The older ones squirmed in their seats, unable to understand what was happening around them but absorbing the nervous tension in the room and making it their own.

In the hallway just outside the lecture hall, DK stopped Travis and handed him a video-cassette tape. "Take this to the FBI agent outside, just like you did with the letter."

"But," Travis said and then stopped.

"But, what?" DK asked. "Aren't you my trusted messenger? Aren't you my special friend? I need you, Triple-T. You're the only one I can trust with this. There is no other."

Travis nodded and took the videotape. Outside the building, he delivered it cautiously to the same FBI agent he'd given DK's previous handwritten missive. At least he thought it was the same agent; he had difficulty distinguishing them from each other. With the tape delivered, Travis returned to the building, passing by Carter Ahntholz and Goyathlay Hernandez who remained on guard at their posts with their weapons.

DK was already addressing the group when Travis returned. "I am not a young man anymore," He was telling them. "But I'm not yet an old man either. I've lived thirty-three years upon this earth. Thirty-three years on this earth, in this life. When I began my work there was a radiant word for us: Joy. And it was sweet. Sweeter than honey. Sweeter even than the Shekhinah glory. But those sweet words turned bitter and the manifestation of God on this earth, once so visible to us, faded. And the sun was obscured from my sight for many days."

"But this is the pattern of the world. This is what they've done again and again. The righteous prophets were mocked and ignored and, in the end, put to death. And we are not surprised. In fact we take pride in it—if we may be allowed such a dubious emotion. You must be coldblooded in order to be rational like this. I have become a *persona non grata* in this world. I am ready to be executed like the Son of God, Jesus of Nazareth. Jesus the Christ. I'm willing to be assassinated just like him."

"There's no chance of leaving now," he continued. "They've already hardened their hearts. They've turned their faces against us and stiffened their necks. So it's inevitable. We will die. I'm sorry to say it. But I will tell you this: We don't have to accept the death that they are offering. We know that we must die, and that's okay. We are ready to die. But we don't have to take the death that they would deal to us. There is another way, a more noble way. We will die, but we can choose the manner of our death. It is still in our power to die bravely and in a state of freedom."

Quiet murmurs rumbled through the room. A few of the women and the smaller children wept. The men bore it all with a silent stoicism but their red and swollen eyes betrayed their fears and their tears too.

"This," DK continued, gradually building the fervor and intensity of his rhetoric. "This will be our sacrifice, the bringing of our bodies, our living bodies, to the flames. We bring ourselves to the altar of this moment. But it is also our Wormwood, our gall. This will not be pleasant. This will not be gentle or genteel. It will be bitter. For many of you it will not feel like comfort. You are fearful. I know it. I see it in the way your eyes are large and wide and following me back and forth across the platform here. I see it in the way you clutch your children and stroke their hair. And I understand. I've been right there with you. I know that fear. I know that terror. But you must walk though those flames to get to the glory on the other side. This is our passion, but it is also our power and our glory."

"Listen people. Here we are, less than a hundred miles from the city of Phoenix, and this is no coincidence. We are here in the shadow of Phoenix, a city named for that great, mythical bird that lives for three, four, five hundred years and then bursts into flames and dies. It burns up. And all that's left of that great bird is ashes. But after just a few days the Phoenix rises up again, new born from the ashes. It lives again and so will we."

"And they will remember us forever. The world will hear the name Zion's Freedom and they will remember that although we gave up our lives we never gave up our freedom. They will remember us and what we do here. And the angels in heaven will commemorate our sacrifice around the throne of God."

"Now there's something that most of you don't know yet, and something that those outside know nothing about at all. For the past several days I've had a crew working, in secret, on something important. Maybe you've seen Gary Matthews and Christoph James and Melvin Schaeffer coming in late, and filthy dirty to dinner. They haven't told you anything about what I've had them doing and you have trusted me enough not to ask them about it either. God bless you, men. I appreciate what you've been doing for me. For all of us. Folks, these men have been working with pickaxes and hammers and shovels to dig us a tunnel that leads from the back trailer to a small cleft and cave in the rock wall behind the compound."

The quiet sobbing amongst the congregation was choked out by audible gasps and whispers of "Hallelujah!" The energy in the room shifted and DK could feel it. His followers were still scared, to be sure. Who wouldn't be with the forces of Babylon arrayed around them, surrounding them and preparing for their deaths. But they were no longer terrorized. Their strength was renewed in a single utterance. Now they would no longer be helpless victims, but instead they would be bold actors, determiners of their own fates.

"Our future with them, with the forces of Hell and Babylon outside, is certain capture. They'll put us in handcuffs and leg irons, and ship us off to prison. They'll take our children away from us. They'll take our precious little boys and girls and deposit them into foster homes and juvenile detention centers. But in that secret place in the shadow of the Most High, in the cleft of the rock, we'll still have the free choice of a noble death. A free death alongside those we hold most dear. The enemies outside want to take us alive, so that they can humiliate and shame us in front of the media. The world would mock us. And if we were to try to fight them, outnumbered and out-gunned as we are, we would soon be taken. They will come through the walls to seize us. You know it as well as I do. We cannot fight them. We have few guns and no matter how many we had, they would never be enough."

"Now don't misunderstand me. These men have been doing hero's work, breaking up and hauling away thousands of pounds of rock and dirt.

But what they have made for us is not an escape tunnel. Gary, Christoph, Melvin, you three have done a tremendous job . . . " DK was forced to stop for a moment as a spontaneous round of cheers and applause from the congregation. "Yes. Yes. Thank you. But it's not a tunnel to freedom. This isn't some Steve McQueen movie. I thought we might have more time to dig further into the mountain. We always knew that the time was short. But it is a tunnel from the compound into the caves in the mountain and that's where we will make our final stand. There in the cleft of the rock. Let the forces of Babylon burst in and take these buildings—we won't be in them. And let them take our bodies—we won't be in them either. We will be gone. We will be free."

* * *

"I wasn't there when DK told everyone about the tunnel. I'd been out delivering the videotape to the FBI. But I knew about it though. He told me what Gary and Melvin and Christoph were doing. I was the one who found the cave and showed it to DK. He just stood there in the entrance to the cave, looking all around and he said, "This is where it all ends.""

"What do you think he meant by that?"

"I didn't know. Not then. I probably could have guessed, I suppose. But I understood him later. And I was ready."

* * *

After the meeting concluded, DK pulled Travis aside. "I've got one more message for you to deliver to the men outside, son."

Travis went out to them, blinking against the bright spotlights trained against the front of the compound as he stepped through the doors. They kept the spotlights on all through the night in an attempt to disrupt and disturb their sleep. But the blackout curtains they'd hung ameliorated the worst of the effects. Travis stepped toward the FBI agents as he had previously, but before he could say anything to them, one of them shouted out. "Sorry, kid. We're going to ask you to turn back around and go inside."

"But I've got a message from the Reverend DK," he told them. "I've got a message to deliver to you."

"I'm sure you do, son. And you've been doing a great job of delivering his messages. You've been calm and brave and you've represented your people well. But we're going to have to speak to the man himself from now on. Tell your reverend that we need to speak to him without an intermediary."

Travis turned, but hesitated and turned back again. "What's a . . . "

"An intermediary is a go between," the FBI agent explained. "Someone who facilitates an agreement between two parties. But from this point forward, we need to speak to the man himself. You've done well, as well as anyone could ask, but we need to speak to your reverend directly now. You go on back inside and let this be the last message that you deliver, son."

A few moments later, after Travis had relayed the FBI message, DK himself stepped through the front doors of the compound. Lit up by the police spotlights, he squinted behind his sunglasses to see the enemies that had surrounded him and his smiled. He loved an audience, friendly or otherwise. "I'm here," he called out to them. "Without an intermediary as you requested. Now there is only one God," he said to them in a clear and loud voice. "And there is only one mediator between God and man . . . "

"Don't give us any more Bible bibble babble, Lewis Earl Howard, or Sixten Johnson, or Reverend DK, or whatever you're calling yourself these days," agent Ramirez interrupted. "We got a whole posse of men out here that just want to see this done without violence. We don't want to see anyone get hurt. We've got a fair and legal warrant for your arrest so just come on out and let's see this done right. No one has to get hurt."

DK smoothed his hair and said, "Well, as the little shepherd boy, David, said to Goliath, the giant champion of the Philistine forces, 'Thou comest against me with a sword, and with a spear, and with a shield, but I come to thee in the name of the Lord of Hosts, the God of the armies of Israel, who thou has defied.'"

Agent Ramirez sighed and said, "Knock off the Bible study, DK, and just tell us what it is that you want."

"Well," he said. "If you can get a bus for the children and their mothers, we'll send them out to you."

Agent Ramirez nodded, obviously relieved. "And what do you want in exchange for the release of these hostages?"

It was DK's turn to sigh now. "You don't understand what's going on here do you? You don't get any of it. I don't want anything in return because they're not my hostages and they're certainly not my prisoners. They came here in freedom, to live and to worship in peace, and they can leave in the same way. Just as freely as they came. I hold no one here against their will."

Taken aback somewhat, Agent Ramirez spoke again. "That's. . . that's mighty fair of you, sir. I'll arrange to have a bus here shortly for your little ones and your women. We can remove them to a place of safety and make sure that they're safe and healthy until all this is sorted out."

"Thank you, agent," DK said. "But don't go to any great trouble to rush yourself about it. We ask for an hour or two so that we might, like the Israelites before the Pharaoh of Egypt, ask for some time to worship our God and to pray together."

"That's fair. That's fair," the agent agreed. "It's going to take at least an hour, maybe longer, to arrange a bus and a driver, anyway. Can we agree on two hours for you and yours to have your prayer meeting and then we'll take your children and your women to safety. After that you'll surrender yourself to the law enforcement officers with the legal warrant? Are we agreed?"

"We are agreed," DK said. "I'll send Travis back out in a few minutes with a list of the children's names and ages and the names of their mothers." He turned toward the door to reenter the compound but the agent stopped him.

"No, hang on a moment there, DK. Hold up," the agent called to him. DK whirled around to face the law enforcement agents again. His eyes were wild behind the sunglasses. "Don't bother sending the boy back out here to deliver your messages. You've got to stop hiding behind the kid, DK. You have to do your own work here. Own up to your responsibilities. Face the situation yourself. Don't send Travis out in your place."

DK glared at them, looking up and down the line of officers with spotlights and firearms pointed at him. He nodded curtly before turning back toward the doors of the compound. But he stopped short of the doors and turned around to speak to the FBI agents again. "One more thing before I go back inside to be with my family. Just one quick question. Do you know the films of Charlie Chaplin? They're quite old."

"I have little time for entertainment," agent Ramirez said patiently.

"No doubt. No doubt. I'm sure that you are a busy man with many and varied demands for your attention. But this might interest you. Charlie Chaplin made films at the beginning of the film age. He was a comedian, famous in his time and still today. He said something that I think about when I'm preaching. He said that 'It is paradoxical that tragedy stimulates the spirit of ridicule. Ridicule is an attitude of defiance. We must laugh in the face of our helplessness against the forces of nature, or go insane.' You might think about carving out a couple of hours to watch one or two of Chaplin's films, agent Ramirez, and you too, agent Marcus," he said over agent Ramirez's shoulder to the other FBI agent standing nearby. "You both might find them amusing, and educational too." With that DK turned around again and entered through the doors of the compound.

Agent Marcus approached his partner and spoke to him. "What was all that Charlie Chaplin stuff? I don't get it."

"I don't know, man. I don't know."

"The guy's crazy. Should we track town some of his films, see what he's going on about?"

"No," agent Ramirez said. "It's just more of his nonsense. Forget it. Let's get that bus." The two of them turned back to the command center to begin working on securing a bus to transport the women and children to safety.

Once DK was safely back inside the buildings of the compound, he was mobbed by his followers who'd been listening to his conversation with the FBI agents. "You're going to send them away? You're going to break up our families?" they all clamored at once. "You're going to give yourself up to them?"

"No. No. No," he said. "It's a stalling tactic. That's all. Nothing more. No one is going anywhere. We will not, any of us, be slaves to them. We will not surrender our little ones. We will not give away our wives. And I certainly will not give myself to them. Not in this life." He could still see the confusion and fear in their eyes, so he said to them, "You trust in God. Trust also in me. Everything will be all right."

"We're going to die, aren't we?" whispered one of the mothers.

"We're all going to die. Everyone everywhere dies," DK answered her. "But we do not fear. There is no death and there are no dead." He kissed her on the cheek and retreated to his private rooms.

* * *

"He told us it was something like a Catholic thing."

"What's that?" Myron asks me.

"DK. He told us that in the Roman Catholic Church, when one of their blessed objects—like their robes, or their altar cloths, or chalices, or rosaries, or medals, or whatever, when they're torn, or worn out, or broken and unusable anymore they have to be burned, or melted down. You can't just throw them out."

"Yes. Or poured directly into the ground, as is the case with holy water. The sacramentals are signifiers, objects of grace. And they have to be treated with special care."

"Yeah. That's the word he used—sacramentals. He said it was like that. Just like that. We're not Catholic, with all their superstitions and idolatry, he said, but it still holds true. The blessed objects aren't disposable. They have to be treated with respect and dignity appropriate to their holy use. When they can't be used anymore they have to be burned. That's what he said. Burned. And he told us that we were like those blessed objects. That we were not disposable things to be thrown away like trash. We were holy. And we could not be treated like trash. We would burn."

* * *

"In this life," DK told them, "In this life, only the wicked can be happy. We are the unhappy outsiders. We are strangers, alienated from society. Jesus told us that in this life we would be hated. And you know the truth of it. You don't need me to tell you. You need only look out the window to see them with their guns, and their cruisers, and their spotlights—all the technologies of their hatred. Truly in this life, only the wicked can be happy."

They were gathered around him in the meeting room, sitting as close as they could to him, some sitting on the floor at his feet. They held their children in their arms and soothed them quiet. The room was deathly still. They listened to the rise and fall of his every salient word.

"We will never be happy here. We will never be at home here. But we shouldn't expect to be happy here—this is not our home."

We are being weighed against eternal immutable values. *Mene, mene, tekel, upharsin*, as the hand of God might have written on the wall. And our lives, weighed in that balance, have value, have weight. But not here. In this world we are worthless. Weightless."

"So now we come to it, my friends, my dear ones. Now we come to the bitter moment when we must decide. Do we want to live the life that this world would lay out for us? A life of struggle. A life of antagonism. A life of rejection. This is what the world would lay out for us. But there is another life. This life is not the only life."

"I know this moment is frightening. It's bitter and it's scary. But this life is too small for ones like you and me. We are destined for a bigger life, a brighter, better life beyond all the pain and misfortune of this world. And that life they cannot take from us. In that life they cannot threaten the small, soft bodies of your children. In that life they cannot break up your homes. In that life they cannot beat you down or break your bones."

"You have to ask yourself: What do you want? What do you want for your kids? Do you want them to be subject to the cruelty and violence of this world? You know that they're out there right now, the agents of Babylon, who've come to take away your babies. They're right outside the gates like some sort of wild, dangerous beasts. They're like a growling, prowling lion waiting to snatch your babies from your arms, ready to devour them with sharp, piercing teeth. Is that what you want? Would you consent to continue in this life knowing that is the inevitable future?"

They shook their heads in response but said nothing. There was nothing to be said. These battered saints of God had no words to unravel the tightly knotted ball of their infirmities. Mere words could not touch it. These were groanings too deep for words, groanings which could not be uttered with fallible human lips and trembling human tongues. The Spirit would speak for them and the prophet would lead them into the will of God They trusted that he would lead them, even into the flames.

* * *

"Tell me how it all went down that night, Travis," Myron says to me.

"I don't know how to begin." I say. After all these hours of talking, I'm still not sure how to begin. "What do you want to know?"

"The medical examiner reports from the Zion's Freedom case show that the members of your group died of gunshot wounds before the fire. Can you tell us who pulled the trigger and how the fire was started? How did your friends meet their end? Did they say anything? Did anyone change their mind and want to leave before the end?"

"No," I tell Myron. "No one wanted to leave the compound. They only wanted to leave this life."

"And you, why did you not leave this life with them?"

"DK told me that I had to live."

"Why? Why did he want you to survive? Why didn't he want you to escape with the others?"

I knew Myron would ask this question eventually. But I do not know how the answer. I loved DK and trusted him, but I never understood. It's not like he gave me a message to share—even though he called me his special messenger. Maybe he thought I was different than the others, but I don't know how. I mean, he could have let me go with them. He could have let me go with him at the end. But instead, I'm still here and I don't know why.

"How did it happen, Travis? Can you tell me that? How did the end begin?"

"Everyone gathered in the Bible study room," I tell him. "They were sitting by family groups. Moms and dads together with their children. DK had everyone's names in a jar and after he said a prayer he drew the names out to determine the order."

"Who went first?" Myron asks me.

"It was Gideon and Janice."

"The Lamonts?" Myron asks.

"Yeah. The ones with the lizard. They'd let Sheila go. Slipped her out one of the windows so that she could escape before everything came down. When DK called Gideon's name, he and his wife stood up together, holding hands, and hugged each other. And then they hugged the people sitting next to them. Everyone was crying but no one seemed sad. It was sorta' strange how calm everyone was. I mean, considering what they were about to do."

"What happened then?"

"DK handed Gideon a flashlight and one of the pistols. Then they went down the hall to the room where the tunnel had been dug back into the cave in the cliff."

"What room was that?"

"It had been a pantry behind the cafeteria. The men who dug the tunnel moved all the shelves and the food out into the hallway so that they'd have room to work."

"So Gideon and Janice went down through the tunnel into the cave in the cliff face. What happened next?"

"After a few minutes we could hear the muffled shot. Gideon used the pistol to shoot her in the back of the head. He laid her body out and then he came back through the tunnel and waited in the refectory for the next family. He handed the flashlight and the pistol off to them. That's how they did it, one family at a time. It got kinda' crowded in there by the end, so they had to start stacking some of the bodies to make room for everyone."

"And the police and the FBI agents outside didn't hear the gunshots?" Myron asks.

"The gun wasn't really loud, and it was far back inside the cave. Plus they were playing music outside. Rock music through big speakers. I think they were trying to use psychological warfare or something on us. But they didn't understand what was happening inside, so they didn't hear the gunshots."

"Who was left after this?"

"After the first round of names were drawn we were down to Gideon Lamont, John Hawkins, Josh Zamecnik, Gary Matthews, Melvin Schaeffer, Carter Ahntholz, Mark Kemper, Emmett Fischer, Goyathlay Hernandez, DK, and me, and Ms. Snow and Gracie."

"Why were Ms. Snow and Gracie left to the end?"

"I don't know. DK said it was just a random drawing. He refilled the jar with the names of the people who still remained and started drawing again. He drew two names—Gary Matthews and Mark Kemper. Mark took Gary down into the cave and shot him. Then DK drew another name—Emmett—and Emmett went down and shot Mark. And so on."

There is a loud buzzing sound and a heavy, metallic clang as the door to the room where this interview is being held opens. One of the prison guards enters and tells Myron that we have ten minutes to finish up. Myron thanks him and then tells me to continue. But suddenly I don't want to say anymore.

"Travis, tell me what happened to Maggie Snow and her daughter."

"I think I want to go back to my cell," I say.

"Travis, please. We're almost done here. Tell me what happened to Maggie and Gracie."

* * *

"Maggie Snow," DK read the name from the jar he held, though it was unnecessary. She and her daughter were the only ones remaining. Maggie stood and brushed her daughter's hair. She kissed her on the forehead and then went down into the cave where she received the pistol from Josh Zamecnik. Josh closed his eyes and nodded. Then Maggie put a bullet into the back of his head. She laid his body atop the others already lying dead in the cave.

Back in the dining area, DK turned and looked at Travis and said, "You know what you need to do now, don't you, son?" Travis nodded and took Gracie by the hand.

"It's going to be dark down there," he told her.

"I'm not scared," she said.

"We're going to see your mom one more time and then . . . " Travis' voice clenched and he couldn't finish speaking. He tried again. "We're going to . . . " But the words choked in his throat.

Gracie took his hand and smiled and whispered to him, "It's okay, Travis. I'm not scared. It's only blood."

The two of them clambered through the tunnel into the cave where Maggie stood waiting for the two of them. She was crying. "Close your eyes," she said to the girl. Then she handed the pistol to Travis. The report of the gunshot was louder here inside the cavern, but Gracie didn't flinch. Her body dropped slowly, limply to the ground. Maggie said nothing, only watched as Travis scooped up her lifeless body and placed it atop the other bodies in the small cave. He smoothed her hair and kissed her on the forehead. "Goodbye, Gracie," he said.

"There was more I wanted to say," Travis said as he turned to face Maggie in the dim glow of the flashlight. "And I had something I wrote for you. I wanted to share it with you but there wasn't time."

"I know." She said. "Do what you have to do, Travis."

"I love you, Ms. Snow."

"Thank you, Travis. I love you too." She closed her eyes and waited for the bullet.

* * *

"At your trial . . . ," Myron beings but he stops and starts again. "You were tried as an adult even though you were only fourteen years old at the time. Arizona statute says that anyone who commits certain types of felonies as juveniles between the ages of fourteen and seventeen can face charges as an adult. You were tried as an adult for the murder of Maggie and Gracie Snow. Do you want to say anything about that?"

"No, I say quietly. "I just want to go back to my cell."

"Your lawyer entered a *nolo contendrere* plea—no contest. Why? Why didn't you plead not guilty?"

I don't answer him. What can I say? What could I say now, after all these years?

"Some have said that Herman Hunter, the district attorney who prosecuted your case, was just too eager for a conviction in the wake of such an awful tragedy and that he didn't take proper time to investigate what happened, and that he should have taken into account your mental condition. They say that there is no righteous reason you should have been tried as an adult."

I know what he's saying even if he doesn't say it. He thinks I'm simple. That I'm slow. That I'm dumb. "I'm not retarded. And I ain't stupid. People have said that about me all my life, but it's not true."

"No. Of course not, Travis. And I apologize. I believe that the term your lawyer used was 'cognitive delay.'"

"I know what that means," I say. "It means I learn slow. I'm not retarded."

"Speak to me, Travis. Help me understand." Myron sounds as if he's begging and suddenly I'm not angry anymore. I feel sorta' bad. But I don't want to say any more. I don't want to talk about Ms. Snow. I don't want to tell him about the whimpering sound she made just before I pulled the trigger. I don't want to think about her, or Gracie, or DK, or any of the others from Zion's Freedom anymore. I'm tired and I just want to go back and lay down on my bunk in my cell.

"And you've never, not once in the last thirty years, applied for parole. Why not? Apart from you, death and destruction are DK's only legacy. Why are you still protecting his memory?"

I say nothing.

"You've spent most of your life in the federal correctional facility here n Phoenix. You've been eligible for parole for many years. And the warden says that you've been a model prisoner—that you've never caused any problems for the other inmates or the guards. If you had applied for parole, it's quite possible that you could have been free by now. Is this the life that your Reverend DK intended for you? Is this what you want?"

I say nothing.

"Did you think that you deserved to be punished? Do you still think you deserve this?"

I say nothing. I have nothing to say.

"Travis? Travis?"

Travis crawled slowly back through the tunnel from the cave into the cafeteria building. He turned off the flashlight and threw it back down the hole from which he emerged. Then he wiped the dirt and blood from his face and hands, smearing it on his pants. He saw the Reverend DK sitting at one of the tables in the refectory eating from a large carton of vanilla ice cream.

"Want some?" he said waving his hand toward the open carton on the table. Melting ice cream dripped from the sides creating a sticky puddle on the table.

"No," Travis said desultorily. He stood, staring off into space, half listening to the music being blared by the police outside.

"This is going to be my last meal. Thought I'd make it something good." DK chuckled and took another large bite of ice cream. "And I've always loved vanilla. Just plain vanilla. Chocolate is good too, but I'll always come back for vanilla. I don't need anything crazy like Rocky Road or caramel. Just give me a scoop of plain old vanilla and I'm happy. Are you sure you don't want any? It's just going to go to waste if we don't eat it," DK said. He ate another bite and then said, "Sit with me, Triple-T."

"Okay," Travis said as he sat down across from DK at the table. He set the pistol on the table between them and waited in silence as DK finished his last meal.

Finally DK pushed the empty ice cream carton away and set down his spoon. "Thought I would have something to say when this moment finally came. I thought I'd have some words of wisdom to pass on to you, my friend. But now that we come down to it, I realize that there's nothing more I can say. I've taught you all that I could teach you. And you know everything that you need to know."

"They'll say that I lied. They'll say 'He fooled everyone, didn't he?' They'll say that I fooled them all because they wanted to believe. But reality is only a construct. An artifice. It's not my fault if they were beguiled. Mesmerized. They'll say that I was a conman with a Bible in one hand, a newspaper in one, and a shotgun in the other. But that's three hands, isn't it Travis?"

He paused and wiped his eyes before he continued. "Someday what's happened here will all make sense. Someday you'll understand all of what

I've said here, and all the things I left unsaid. And when that day comes, you'll know what you need to do."

Travis nodded and stared into DK's eyes.

"Goodbye, Triple-T." DK picked up the pistol, took a deep breath, stuck it into his mouth and pulled the trigger. But there was no bullet, no recoil, no report. Just a small click as the hammer came down on an empty chamber. DK dropped the gun back on the table and said with a mirthless chuckle, "It figures, doesn't it? That's just the way it would go. You come to the end and it's empty." He laughed again and then said, "I'm going to need you to get the shotgun for me, Travis."

Travis stood and went to find the shotgun for his friend and teacher.

"I've thought of something," DK said when the boy returned with the weapon. "So I guess it's a good thing that the pistol was empty. I've thought of something I want to say to you before I leave you and the rest of this crazy world."

"What is it?" Travis asked as he handed the shotgun across the table to DK.

"We've come to it now. The end, Triple-T. This is the end. I thought that I wouldn't be afraid. I thought that I was done with fear. But now that it's here, like this, I am afraid. And I'm afraid this is the last thought that I will have before I die. This is the last thought I will have before I die." He looked into Travis' eyes one last time and said, "This is the last thought I will have before I die. This is the last thought I will have before I die. This is the last thought I will have before I die."

Before Travis could ask DK what that meant, DK put the shotgun under his chin and pulled the trigger. There was a fierce blast and the top of his skull was blown away. Blood, bone, and brain sprayed across the room. The shotgun fell to the floor still smoking. DK's body collapsed in a pool of blood.

* * *

"Okay, Travis. If you won't say anything more about the deaths of Maggie Snow and her daughter, will you tell me something about DK's death? The evidence remaining after the fire suggested that he died by a self-inflicted gunshot wound, but that was contested by the district attorney. He wanted to try you for his death as well, didn't he?"

I nod.

"Did you do it?"

"No," I say. "He left me . . . " I stop and begin again. "He left this world on his own."

"You still miss him, don't you?" Myron asks. And it's true that I do. He was the father I never had and a friend. I miss him more than I could ever say. So I say nothing.

A loud buzzer sounds and the metal door opens with a clang again. A guard steps enters the room and tells Myron that our time is up and that I have to return to my cell now. I stand to follow him out. But before I do, I have one more question for Myron. "Why did God not . . . " But I can't finish the question. I'm not entirely sure what it is I want to ask.

"What, Travis? Why did God not what? What is it you want to ask?" He seems desperate to know. But I just wave and turn back toward the guard.

"Travis, one more thing before you go," Myron says as I'm leaving.

"What?" I say at the door.

Myron falters and I realize that he doesn't actually have another question prepared. Here at the end he just doesn't know what he should say. I smile at him. "Thank you," he says instead of asking another question. He stands and sticks out his hand as if to shake mine, but the guard disapproves. "No touching," he barks. No physical contact is allowed in the correctional facility. Myron retracts his hand awkwardly and says to me, "I appreciate your candidness, Travis. You've been entirely forthright." I nod and that is it. I turn and leave the room.

* * *

The compound was on fire, the buildings, the trailers ablaze and the flames were spreading to the watchtower. The blue starred flag of Zion's Freedom began to burn as it fluttered in the updraft created by the heat of the fires. Back, acrid smoke billowed high into the sky.

"No one's coming out," the law enforcement officers outside began to whisper among themselves. "No one's coming out! No one's coming out!" they shouted.

The complex was engulfed in black, choking chemical smoke. Smoldering Bible pages fluttered in the air with drifting embers and bits of soot. Rifle rounds began to explode from somewhere inside the compound. By the strange physics of fire, flames were sucked down through the tunnel into the small death chamber carved into the side of the mountain and the bodies of the dead began to burn.

There were no screams from inside the compound, no sound of crying children or weeping mothers. There were no shouted commands from the law enforcement agents surrounding. There was only an eerie, disquieting stillness as the fire consumed the structure.

Travis walked out of the burning compound, with flames roaring up behind him. He held his arms above his head as the SWAT team rushed forward and tackled him. He was handcuffed and dragged to the back of a squad car beyond the barricades.

Epilogue

A FEW DAYS AFTER this interview was completed, Travis Thompson Took, known to some as Triple-T, hung himself in his prison cell using a rolled up plastic trash bag as a noose. The guard who found him reacted immediately to cut him down and attempted CPR, but Travis was already dead. He was pronounced dead by suicide by the medical examiner. There is much more that we would have liked to have asked and many questions that remain unanswered. He left no note and no explanation. He wrote no memoir, and gave no other interviews.

He left only a terrible silence.

www.ingramcontent.com/pod-product-compliance
Lightning Source LLC
Chambersburg PA
CBHW060425260626
47161CB00005B/1791